Four Sisters

by

Glenn Willis Pace

DORRANCE
PUBLISHING CO
EST. 1920
PITTSBURGH, PENNSYLVANIA 15238

Dorrance Publishing Co
701 Smithfield Street
Pittsburgh, PA 15222
Visit our website at *www.dorrancebookstore.com*

ISBN: 978-1-4809-2660-8
eISBN 978-1-4809-2798-8

Prologue

The meeting took place at one of Los Angeles' plushest and oldest hotels on the thirteenth floor. It lasted one hour.

The President of BOAS (Brotherhood of America's Salvation) brought the meeting to order. Inside Suite 1313, there were thirteen members, some of the most powerful people in the United States of America. Twelve of the thirteen members were standing to the left of their numbered high-backed chair. The chairs were made of walnut, and covered with white leather. The armrests were covered with white leather and white suede, with a number carved into them. Each number represented the order of power and wealth, with one being the least powerful to thirteen being the most powerful. In order to be a member of BOAS, you would have to have at least 500 million dollars in petty cash. Each member represented a necessity of life—gas, oil, electric, precious metals, real estate, stocks and bonds, labor and industries, education, law, health, and politics.

The six men and six women, who were all dressed in black attire from head to toe, were standing at opposite sides of a solid oak, v-shaped, thirteen-foot long table. The suite was dimly lit, except for the thirteen lamps (each made of gold and pewter) sitting in front of their marked places. The thirteen members were not the type of individuals that regular working people would want to piss off; unfortunately, one person had done just that, and the only problem was that the person didn't even know it.

The President of BOAS, who was called Thirteen, walked into the suite and took his place at the very tip of the v-shaped table and sat down. Being the leader of BOAS, Thirteen is the only member who is dressed entirely in white. As Thirteen sat down, the other members sat down in order of their number. Thirteen addressed the group. "We all agreed at our last meeting that we don't want that person in office, so we have contracted a group of people to help us with an out. Payment is 26 million dollars, half now and the other half when the contract is fulfilled. I have invited a member of the group to speak at our meeting. Ms. Cancer, would you please come in?"

Cancer opened the door and walked into the meeting. Cancer was a voluptuous five-foot eleven-inch, black-haired, brown-eyed, light brown-skinned Afro-American. Cancer's face was shaped like a pear with a sharp chin and smooth as a polished pearl. She was wearing a two-piece, plain black velour suit with a light blue blouse with a crab emblem blazed on the upper right-hand corner. Her hair was set in tight braids, pulled to the back, and her boots were high and black, with a crab emblem engraved onto the outer side of each boot. With a tone of self-confidence, Cancer spoke to the members. "BOAS, we the Correctors accept your offer. You have agreed to our fee of 24 million dollars, with a 2 million dollar signing bonus."

Thirteen spoke to Cancer. "Ms. Cancer, we also expect you to make sure that the City of Brotherly Love knows that you mean business. Make your presence known with thirteen days of carnage, as we agreed."

"Whatever turns you on," Cancer replied as she picked up the thirteen white leather and suede envelopes rubber banded together, and walked toward the door.

"With that, one of us shall see you on November 8. Ms. Cancer, break our contract, and we will kill you last."

Cancer turned around and looked Thirteen in his deep-seated, cold, hard-as-steel blue eyes, smiled and replied, "That's funny, that's the same thing we were saying about you." Cancer turned and walked out the door.

"This meeting will reconvene on the November 8; therefore, this meeting is now in recess … until then, good day."

Four
Sisters

"**You** did what?" Taurus bellowed, as Cancer provided the details of their next assignment. "Are you crazy? You took a job order from a bunch of white racists, and on top of that, to take out one of our own? No!"

Cancer shot back at Taurus, the leader of the Correctors. The Correctors are a group of highly-educated, well-trained, and very experienced assassins. "Don't talk about being racist, all we ever do is 'Whitey', so what the hell does that make us?"

Taurus looked at Cancer with contempt in his eyes, because he knew that she was right.

"It doesn't matter," Leo (the second in command) spoke up. The lowlifes that we kill deserve to die. Look, Taurus, we are a group of killers, nothing but a bunch of lowlifes ourselves. The bottom line is we kill people for money and nothing else. It's just another job, that's all."

"Another job," injected Libra.

"But that's not all," Cancer informed the team.

"Can, I'm trying to help you out, don't push it," Libra said.

"The job is in Philly," Cancer mumbled in a low tone.

"You do mean Philly, as in Philly, Mississippi, right, Can? Can?" Gemini 2 asked.

Cancer mumbled, "Philly, as in Philadelphia, PA."

Taurus blew his stack. "She's outta her freaking mind! We can't go to Philly and she knows it. You are going to start a blood bath, Cancer. You've put us in a very serious and very awkward position, young lady," Taurus said, looking at Cancer with his dark eyes and a look of dread and concern.

"Why can't we go to Philly, tell me why? Why can't we go?" Scorpio asked.

"It's because of a stupid twenty-five year-old pact we made," answered Aries.

"Damn, Taurus," said Cancer, "we were young and just starting out; now we are older and more mature, and a lot stronger. We are respected, and even feared by our peers. We are the very best in our field; who in their right mind is going to challenge or cross us? Who 'T'? Who?"

The 'Centaur' that's who," answered Capricorn. "We were wise to make that pact with the Centaur. He stays out of LA; we stay out of Philly."

"Wait a minute," Scorpio said. "What if one of us has family in Philly, does that mean we can't go to see them?"

"No, little one," Taurus answered. "As long as you go to socialize you are okay, but as far as work, it's a no-no. You do know that if we go to Philly, we are breaking the pact and that means taking on the Centaur; and I, for one, am not excited about taking on a brother who was once our leader. And, that's not even talking about the headache that comes along with it; you talk about a migraine…."

"Yeah, you're right, Cap. If we go to Philly and we are forced to take on the Centaur, we won't have any other choice but to take him out of the picture for good," Leo added.

"Yeah, like we are going to have a choice. You know as well as I do, we go to Philly, one or more of us is going to die. The big 'Q' is, how many and who?" Pisces added,

"Don't worry about it, Can; we can go to Philly, do what we have to do, and leave without the Centaur ever knowing we were there," Leo said.

"Our luck is not that good," Gemini 2 stood up responding to Leo. "He did make it clear that if we were to meet under any condition other than social, someone would die."

"Yeah, and your yellow ass will be the first on the list," grinned Cancer.

"After what you did to him, hell yeah, I'd be afraid to go to Philly, too. As for myself, I'd rather take my chances and deal with one homicidal nut than thirteen. Besides, Cancer accepted the contract on behalf of us all, and once we commit, there's no turning back," Gemini 1 spoke out.

"We go to Philly and may God have mercy on our souls," Taurus said. "Tomorrow we start making our plans for the trip." As the group started leaving the meeting, Taurus pulled Gemini 2 to the side. "Listen little girl, I haven't seen the Centaur for over twenty-five years. I don't know what frame of mind he has, nor am I willing to take a chance with your life to find out. So, as long as we are in the City of Brotherly Love, you stick close to me. No wandering around the city by yourself. I can't take the chance of you running into the Centaur by accident or otherwise."

"What do you mean 'T'?"

"I mean the look in your eyes tells me that you still love the Centaur and that makes you dangerous, not only to yourself, but to all of us. If, and only if, we run into the Centaur, be cool."

"What about my kids?"

"If they want to see you, they will, when they are ready and only then, got it?"

"Got it, 'T'."

"Okay. Now go get some sleep; it will be a long day tomorrow. Don't worry about the Centaur; everything will be just fine, I'm looking forward to seeing the girls myself."

•   •   •   •

The next morning the Correctors met to plan their trip to Philadelphia. "So what do we have on file about the Centaur?" Taurus asked Capricorn, who kept all the files updated in case needed.

"Well, at least we don't have to kill him; all we have to do is kidnap one of his four daughters. Then we call him and let him know if he wants her back alive, he will follow our instructions, without letting him know who it is that has her."

"And what will the instruction be?" Libra asked.

"To back off," smiled Capricorn.

"Oh, hell yeah, we're dead ducks," said Virgo.

"Wait; let me get this thing straight," Pisces spoke up. Number 1, we break the pact by going to Philly with hostile intentions. Then number 2, kidnap one of his daughters. Number 3, call and tell that already mad motherfucker to back off while we kill the top politician in his city, and if he doesn't, we will kill his little girl. Oh, hell yeah, he's really going to love that bullshit."

"You are right, 'V'; we are going to die in the City of Brotherly Love. Gemini 2 looked at her club members in sheer horror.

"Close your mouth, Sis; you might get a dick in it," grinned Gemini 1, her older and only sister.

"Fuck you, Teresa!" (Gemini 1's real name), shouted Gemini 2. "Kidnap one of my kids? Are you fucking people out of your minds? That crazy son of a bitch will kill us all for sure then," Gemini snapped.

"Hold on, Tonya," (Gemini 2's real name).

"Hold up, everyone," Capricorn interrupted. "For the benefit of those who do not know, Tonya and the Centaur have four daughters together. And, get a load of this, all four are cops: Tynisha—28, 5'9", 160 pounds—homicide division, on the job seven years; number two, Christina—26, 5'7", 150 pounds—narcotics division, on the job five years; number three, Justina—24, 5'10", 175 pounds—PA state trooper, on the job three years at the State Capitol; and last of all, there is the baby, Tracy—22, 6'2', 200 pounds—on the job one year, beat cop."

"Now what was that about kidnapping one of his children?" Pisces grinned.

"Oh yeah, by the way, they all have degrees in the martial arts—all black belts—I believe second or third degree—so which one you gonna take on, the baby, perhaps?"

"The baby? The baby is the biggest one of all," Leo stated.

"She just might be the easiest one," laughed Aries, falling from her chair onto the floor. Rolling around, grabbing her stomach, tears rolling down her cheeks, "It hurts, it hurts," she said laughing.

"That's not funny, Aries," Leo barked. "What's funny is if the Centaur had anything to do with his daughters' training, and I'm quite sure he did, they will be a handful. And, if any one of those girls…er, young ladies is close to their father, those girls as you call them, man, they will rip us apart if we come attacking their father or die trying. I don't even want to venture down that road."

"Leave my kids alone!" Tonya screamed.

"Yeah, that's right; just leave my niece's alone, because when they catch up with their mommy, they will be too busy kicking her ass to even be bothered with us," smirked Teresa.

"Go to hell, Teresa," Tonya shouted.

"Ain't that a bitch? Because of one man, we are going to have to take on the entire Philadelphia Police Department, and the Pennsylvania State Police. Sounds exciting," grinned Scorpio.

"In addition, what is the Centaur doing these days?" Libra asked.

"Retired from the Philadelphia PD, had two or three mild heart attacks in the last five years. Owns a restaurant-lounge; it keeps him busy. He lives in a section of the city called Chestnut Hill," Capricorn answered.

Taurus looked at Cancer, "Since this is your contract, you, Virgo, Aries, and Libra get packed. Secure our headquarters, and stay out of sight. We'll be there in two weeks."

"How many are we taking, 'T'?" Teresa asked.

"Just Alpha team; we won't or shouldn't need anyone else."

"Six may not be enough, Taurus," Leo stated. Remember that we may have to deal with the Centaur."

"Leo, you may be right. Bravo team will come along, Charlie and Delta will be on standby," Taurus ordered. "And, remember, stay out of sight. Out of sight, out of mind," Taurus commanded.

"Wait a damn minute, Taurus," Tonya snapped. "What about my children, I asked you?"

"What about them, Gem? I don't want them involved in this at all."

"Nobody could be that damn stupid, nobody," Cancer replied.

"Look, stupid, your brats are cops, we are assassins; we are going to Philly to kill somebody, and the cops will come and, if we are caught, they will hang our asses. And, if I can get away by blowing away a handful of cops, I will. And if they just so happen to be one or more your little angels, so be it; got it, you dumb bitch?"

"That's enough," Cancer.

"No, it's not, Taurus," Cancer yelled back. "Stupid ass over here is going to get us all killed with her dumbass self."

"We'll forget about the kids for right now; maybe we will never even come into contact with them. Our biggest worry is our intended target, and that's all right now and nothing else, understand, Gem? So get it out of your mind that we are going to harm your kids, because that kind of shit is crazy, ludicrous; you know that's not what we are about," Taurus assured Tonya.

"Bullshit, 'T', let one of those motherfuckers get in the way of me doing my job, or getting away, and her ass will be going to a funeral…maybe more than one," stated Cancer.

"Cancer, if any one of you touches one… NO, if any one or more of my girls get hurt or killed, I will kill you myself; remember that, whore," Tonya warned Cancer.

"Oh? When that day comes, I am going to enjoy fucking you up," Cancer laughed.

Teresa, who was sitting at a table in the meeting room, was listening to the exchange of words between the two women, mumbled, "That bitch is going to make me kick her pretty black ass all over this city one day, behind fucking with my sister."

Aquarius smiled, looking at Teresa, thinking to himself. *No matter what they think, Teresa loves her sister, and one day it just might cost her a lot, maybe her life.*

Philadelphia

"Good morning, Daddy," Tracy said as she walked into the kitchen nook of her and her father's duplex. Derrick lives on the first floor and Tracy lives on the second. They both share a large kitchen, so they can see each other without Derrick having to climb up the stairs.

"Good morning, baby," he returned the greeting. "Anything exciting on your list today?"

"Nope, not a thing," Tracy grinned. "But I will say this, if you and Shannon don't hurry up and get together soon, I'm arresting you two for disorderly conduct."

"Well, it just so happens that the ADA and I are meeting for lunch today to talk about our future, okay officer?"

"Take her to Elaine's down on South Street, she'll love it."

"You look good in that uniform, kid."

"Thanks, Daddy, I wouldn't have made it if wasn't for you, Shannon, and my big sisters."

"Yes, you would've, honey; all you needed was a little boost." Derrick handed her a cup of black coffee.

"Thank you. Remember, Daddy, Jessie will be home next Friday, and all of us are meeting at the restaurant for dinner; don't forget."

"How can I? By the way, the real estate office called; they've rented out both of the triplexes to a company called the Correctors. They paid a year in advance."

"I have to go, Daddy." Tracy stood up, finished her coffee, kissed Derrick on the cheek, and walked out the door.

As soon as Tracy left, the telephone rang. Derrick stood up and walked over to the window where the phone hung on the wall, and started looking out as he picked up the phone.

"Hello? Hi, Daddy, it's Tiny."

"I haven't gotten that old that I don't know my own kids' voices; not yet, anyway."

"Cut it out, Daddy, how are you?"

"I'm fine, little girl, how are you?"

"I'm good, Daddy."

The conversation lasted fifteen minutes before Tynisha told her father, "Guess what, Daddy?" and before Derrick could answer, she continued. "David proposed to me last night and I said 'yes'."

"That's wonderful, baby, another cop in the family."

"I already told Crissy."

"So what you are telling me is dig deep into my pockets, right?"

"You got it, Pops." They both laughed. "Dad, I'll see you at the bar tonight, okay?"

"Okay, baby, see you tonight."

"Love you, Daddy."

"Love you too, Tiny, so long," Derrick said as he hung up.

Standing, staring out of the window, looking at nothing in particular, he thought aloud how lucky he was to have four girls all follow in his footsteps, who were making it in this madness called life. Single tears rolled down his cheeks as he grinned. Derrick, in his early fifties, was in good shape and health for someone to have had three minor heart attacks in the last five years. Standing at 6'7" even and 230 pounds, his hair, salt and pepper, his body still had telltale signs of his great physical conditioning doing his days as a martial arts student and police officer. Derrick finished his coffee and went to get dressed.

As Derrick dressed, a cold shiver ran through his body. Those apartments cost twelve hundred and fifty dollars a month. He added up the rent for all six apartments for a year, plus security deposits. *It must be a big company*, he thought, shrugging off the feeling and continued dressing.

• • • •

The two triplexes the Correctors had rented were side-by-side in the Mount Airy section of the city. Both were well equipped with a washer and dryer in their basements. Each apartment had two spacious bedrooms, each with air conditioners. The basements were finished, with half the back carpeted. Cancer and Libra would have the first floor of the first apartment building. The Gemini twins would have the second floor, and Aquarius and Scorpio (who were married) would have the third floor. Aries and Virgo (who were soul mates) would share the first floor of the second building. Taurus and Leo would have the second floor, and Pisces and Capricorn shared the third floor. Taurus and Leo, who arrived on Monday, were the last to settle in.

"It's not as big as LA or the 'Big Apple', but it's still big," marveled Leo.

By the end of the week, their equipment began to arrive. That Sunday night, Taurus called a meeting. "Listen up, everybody; we'll make this quick. First, we have exactly twelve weeks here in the City of Brotherly Love. The first four weeks, we stake out our prey. We find out all his daily routines, we find out where he lives, find out family ties, where he eats, sleeps, and so on. We find out everything we could possibly need to know about this guy. The next two weeks, the escape route; we find every exit possible. We will ride every form of transportation they have to offer. We will check out the airports, and any possible water transportation. Last of all, we check out the speed of the taxi service. Check out the different cab companies they have to offer. We do this in teams. Nobody, but nobody, explore any of these systems by themselves. We do this in pairs. Cancer and Libra, you two have the EL system. The twins have the Broad Street line. Aquarius and Scorpio have the trolley lines. Aries and Virgo have the bus system; check out the routes that pertain to our surrounding living area, too. Pisces and Capricorn have the airports. Leo and I will take the taxi services. All of us will check out waterways.

"We do rehearsals and dry runs. After the rehearsals, we mark off our different hit routes. We will have twelve hit spots. For two weeks, we look, find, and mark out your own spot that you are comfortable with. Now understand one thing, the school kids will be going back to school right after Labor Day, so keep that in mind when you pick your hit spot. The very last thing we need or we want is to hurt or kill an innocent child. Don't bullshit around, learn how to get around this city, and learn it well.

"Last, but not least, according to this city map, we are two miles from Chestnut Hill. We are right around, or should I say right down the street from the Centaur. Do not go near or into his place of business. Stay away from Chestnut Hill. I repeat…stay away from Chestnut Hill, and that goes double for you, Tonya. Stay away from the Centaur's place of business, and that means not even to get a look at your daughters."

Tonya stared in shock at Taurus, as she wondered in her mind, *can he read me that well?*

"When the time comes, you will see them, I promise you that, okay? I give you my word."

"Okay 'T', okay," Tonya smiled.

Cancer spoke up, "Listen, I can't stand your little high yellow ass, but I will make sure you see your girls or die trying. I mean, hell, I'm not a mother, but I am a woman, and we have to support each other in some cases, you know what I mean? But, after you see your brats, then I'll kick your ass."

"Thanks, Cancer," Tonya said as she started to softly cry.

Teresa looked at Cancer in shock and mumbled to herself, *just when I'm ready to rip her eyes out, behind my sister, she goes and gets soft on her. I hate that bitch.*

"Okay, after we do our rehearsals, we get two weeks off. So enjoy them, because we go right back to work after that. We have to make sure that everything is Kosher; we do not want to be stuck in this city after doing our job. Finally, yet most importantly, I want a cheesesteak." Everyone laughed. "This meeting is over. Oh, by the way, pick up your prey ID packet on the way out."

•　　•　　•　　•

For four weeks, the Correctors learned how to get around in the city. They rode every form of transportation the city had to offer, including the ferry from downtown Philadelphia to downtown Camden, New Jersey, across the Delaware River. They learned just about everything that could be learned about their prey. At the end of the tiresome four weeks, the Correctors had a meeting in the basement of the first house, which they turned into the main meeting room.

"Man, this city is a whole lot bigger than I thought it was," stated Aries.

Taurus, looking at his tired companions said, "Enough work. Let's go out and party in our host city. I've always wanted to see the Liberty Bell."

"Taurus, can we carry our weapons?" Cancer asked.

"It all depends on where you are going," Taurus responded. "Take me, for instance, I'm going to see the Liberty Bell; I can't carry my piece because of the metal detectors. So, if you think you are going somewhere where they have metal detectors, leave your piece at home. If you are not sure that there is a metal detector, leave your piece here. We do not want to be stopped by a young rookie cop and try to explain why we are carrying a weapon. So, use your own discretion, but remember we don't want or need any unnecessary trouble. Any questions?" Taurus asked. No one answered. "Good, let's go out and enjoy ourselves."

•　　　•　　　•　　　•

It was nine-thirty A.M. when the Correctors left to start their well-earned, two-week vacation. In addition, at the same time, the mayor was just beginning an emergency meeting with his chief of staff and some of the top brass in his administration at the Criminal Justice Center.

"Please, have a seat." Mayor Downs began the meeting. "Good morning." Everyone returned the greeting. "Five o'clock this morning, I received a phone call from Mayor White of Los Angeles. Mayor White informed me that a team of assassins are either on their way or are already here in the city of Philadelphia. According to the mayor, their narcotics squad busted a major drug ring operation and one of the prisoners made a deal with their DA for a favorable recommendation during his sentence. The informant tipped the mayor that a group of assassins wanted by one-third of the free world's law enforcement agencies, are coming here to kill someone important. The informant does not know if the person they are coming here to kill is a man or a woman, or what position that the person carries. These people are responsible for the deaths of…let me see here, I have a list here. Here we are…two mayors, one governor, three senators, four lawyers, two dozen drug dealers, and six of them were highly-protected kingpins. And, eight witness protection clients, while they were still in the program mind you, and that's just the first page of this report the mayor faxed to me. Hell, I haven't even read what they did in the rest of the world, and what I just read to you took place in the last ten years. By the way, they hate law enforcement officers, period. Neither race nor sex matters to them. In the twenty-five years that they have been operating, they have been linked to forty cops killed in the line of duty, from the states of WA, OH, CA, TX, WY, OK, AR, NM, OR, NY, NJ, DE, and MA. All thirteen of those states have been trying to catch these people, but to no avail. However, what makes matters worse…no one knows who these people are. There are no known photos, no fingerprints…nothing, nothing at all. We are clueless as to how to catch them or when they are going to strike. Los Angeles police had two of them cornered in a dead end alley one early morning after killing a well-known and well-protected drug lord. The drug lord had six, I repeat, six highly trained, heavily-armed bodyguards. Not only did they kill the drug lord, but all six bodyguards, too. By the time back up arrived, the two suspects were not only long gone, but also left four cops dead. Two of the cops' necks were broken, and all four were killed with their own service weapons. People, these are assassins. They do not care who they kill or their sex or age; if they have a contract on you, you are dead.

"Our problem is we don't know who these people are, if they are here, who they are after, or when they are acting. So, as of right now, we go on level one alert. I'm doing this as a safety precaution measure only. We do not need to inform the public and start a citywide state of panic. We have an election coming up in eight weeks, and all we need is for the front-runner to be killed by a bunch of lunatics. If that were to happen, we all would have to go to Libya; our chances of staying alive would be a whole lot better. I want double and 'round the clock protection for Waters, whether he likes it or not.

"The last two items…one, every time these people strike, they leave a calling card. Zodiac signs are on the cards. So far, twelve cards have been found."

"That's all twelve Zodiac signs, sir," the mayor's chief of staff pointed out."

"Not quite," said the mayor.

"I don't understand, sir."

"It's like this…true, twelve cards have been found, but only eleven signs are accounted for. Gemini is the sign of twins."

"So, which sign hasn't been accounted for, then?" Police Commissioner James Lomb asked. The ninth sign," Mayor Downs answered, "Sagittarius. I want to know why no one has found that sign."

"My second and last item. Some of the assassins are women. This meeting is to go only as far as your divisions; inform your commanders that they are not to disclose anything about the alert or the potential threat. If anyone disobeys the order, he or she will be fired immediately. Please pick up the briefing packet on the way out." "Everyone have a good day."

The mayor walked out of the meeting room and everyone else followed, going their separate ways. Walking down the hall, the mayor thought to himself, *God have mercy on our souls.*

•   •   •   •

Christina was sitting at her desk at the South Division Narcotics Headquarters, doing paperwork when Debra Carver-Jenkins came in and sat down at her desk facing the desk of her lifelong best friend, Christina Jenkins. Debra just stared at Christina. "Must I remind you that I have a loaded 9-mm, and I'm not afraid to use it?" Debra said nothing. "He was nice, sweet, handsome, and married."

Her best friend of twenty years looks at Christina in shock. "Married? That fine, long-legged, sweet-smelling son of a bitch is married?"

"Yes, and with six, mind you, six kids."

"Oh shit, Crissy, I'm sorry." Wait until I get my hands on that piece of shit."

"Yeah, well, you're going to have to wait a while for that."

"Why?"

"He had an outstanding warrant, so I got my revenge for him being so fine and so fucked-up. Thanks, Deb, I really needed that."

Debra sunk low into her chair and whispered, "Sorry. What's the warrant all about?"

Both women looked at each other for about five seconds and at the same time say, "Child support," and started laughing.

"Jenkins, Carver-Jenkins, the captain wants to see you two, now," a uniformed officer informed the two women.

"Thanks," Debra responded.

"Okay, bitch, what have you done now?" Christina asked.

"Not me, you horny, can't-get-a-man slut," Debra shot back as they began to gently push each other on their way to the captains' office.

Inside Captain David Daniels' office, he instructed both detectives to have a seat, and both sat down. Captain Daniels is a 6'2", 175-pound, part Irish, part German, ex-pro football player. He has green eyes and a full crop of salt and pepper hair. *His half-moon shaped face is as smooth as a baby's ass*, thought Christina, as she was looking at him while waiting for him to speak. Just looking at his forearms, you can tell he is in good shape for a man of sixty years in age.

"Jenkins, are you with us?" Daniels asked Christina.

"Don't mind her, Captain, she's just a little horny…oops, I mean a little edgy."

"Bitch!" Christina responded.

"Hell, don't get mad at me because you haven't been laid in two years, slut.

Christina nudged Debra in the side. "Hey, Captain, you're single, want a date?"

"I'm going to kick your ass," Christina told Debra, while blushing.

"Knock it off, you two," Daniels told the two women.

"Hell, Captain, that's what I'm trying to get you to do, knock it off."

"Oh, I'm going to kill you, you lowlife," Christina told Debra.

"Noo! That's what your date was last night," Debra interrupted, smiling at Christina.

"Wait until we get out of here, bitch, I'm going to…."

"Stress, see all the stress, Captain? And I have to work with this every day," Debra again interrupted, shoving back.

"I said, knock it off, and if you say one more word, you'll be walking a beat in uniform by this afternoon, got it, Carver-Jenkins?" the captain yelled.

"Got it, sir," Debra replied. "You two clowns are being assigned temporarily to a special task force being assembled as we speak. The commander of the task force in this sector is Tynisha Jenkins. Have you two ever worked with your sister?"

"No, sir," Both women answered.

"Well, she will give you two the details. But, remember where you two come from."

"Meaning what, Captain?" Debra asked.

"Meaning sometimes Eighth Street gets carried away and reassigns cops to other divisions after the task force is over; that's how your sister wound up in Homicide," Daniels said, looking at Christina. "Be at Eighth Street (police headquarters) at fourteen hundred hours tomorrow; that's all."

The two left. Once back at their desks, "I wonder what this is all about."

"We'll find out tomorrow," Debra responded.

•   •   •   •

Police headquarters:
The briefing lasted a little over two hours. Christina and Debra were paired together. Tracy Jenkins was assigned to communications, which she didn't care for at all, and after the meeting, she let her sister know how she felt... for all the good it did. Tynisha told her she either take the position that was given to her or find another job. Tracy was angry with her big sister. Like it or not, they were now a part of PERT (Police Emergency Response Team), a one thousand personnel unit. The state police also had a briefing and Justina was reassigned from highway patrol to Capitol Hill to help guard the first family. Like her sister Tracy, she was not happy; she was very upset, but for different reasons than Tracy. She had her vacation cancelled, and she was looking forward to seeing her father and sisters again. At both of the briefings, the last thing all the officers were told was, they were not to mention the task force or the potential threat to anyone, and that meant not even to their families, or friends. Disobeying the order would result in immediate termination.

•   •   •   •

The Correctors were into the second week of their two-week vacation, and they were enjoying themselves, touring historic downtown Philadelphia. They visited Liberty Mall (where the Liberty Bell is housed), Betsy Ross's house, Elfreth's Alley, Edgar Allen Poe's home, Ben Franklin's grave, Congress Hall, Independence Hall, and Love Park. They took a tour of City Hall; by the time they were on their last two days of vacation, they had toured half the city. The Correctors even went to Atlantic City by Greyhound bus. There was no mention of what they were in Philadelphia to do.

On the last night of their vacation, the Correctors decided to split up and go their own way for the rest of the evening. "Remember, we are here to do a job, and that means to stay out of trouble. And that goes double for you, Aquarius, and I mean it," barked Taurus. "Everybody have their piece on them?" Everyone nodded 'yes'.

"Keep an eye on your husband, Scorp," Leo added.

"Not me," Scorpio replied, "I'm going to bed; this city may not be as big as LA or NY, but it's still big."

"Are you going in with your wife?" Leo asked Aquarius.

"No, not yet, I'm going to walk around a little while." Looking at his wristwatch, Aquarius stated, "It's only six-thirty."

"Baby, pick up one of those sandwiches. What's the name of those things?"

He mumbled, "Hoagies."

"Would you get me a ham hoagie and an iced tea?"

"I'll be in by eleven."

"Aquarius, baby, stay away from the cops," Scorpio pleaded with her husband.

"Okay, okay," Aquarius responded.

Everyone went his or her own separate way. After walking around about six blocks on Chestnut Street, Aquarius hailed a cab. The Yellow Cab stopped in front of him and he gets in.

"Where to, dude?" the young black driver asked.

"Seventeenth and Allegheny Ave.," Aquarius read off a piece of paper he pulled from his suit jacket, left breast pocket."

After riding in silence for about ten minutes, the cab pulled up to a corner and stopped. "Seventeenth and Allegheny Ave., my brother. That's twelve even, dude."

"Okay, dude," Aquarius responded, handing the young, cocky driver a fifty-dollar bill.

"Hey, man! I don't have change for that," he cried out.

"I didn't ask you for change, did I? You just meet me back here at this very spot at ten-thirty and there's a hundred waiting for you, okay, dude?"

"I'll be back at ten-fifteen, dude."

After getting out of the cab, the driver pulled off, and Aquarius walked down the street, stopping at the first bar he came to. He looked at the red and black painted sign on the door, BLACK JACKS ARE WILD. He opened the door and walked in. The first thing he noticed was that the bar had a fresh floral scent, like roses. It was clean and well kept. He also noticed the walls were painted baby blue and lined with different glass-enclosed pictures of famous people. The wall was covered with all types of famous people. Underneath the pictures were open booths where there were seats for two or four people. There were five ceiling fans, of which only two were operating. The bar itself was long and separated into three sections. It being only seven o'clock, two of the sections were closed. There were five people total sitting at the bar—three women and two men. Each had a drink sitting in front of them, except for one; she was working on a crossword puzzle.

She looked up from the paper and asked, "Can I get you something?"

Aquarius walked to the bar near the woman and sat three stools down from her. "Scotch on the rocks and a beer," he replied.

The woman got up and walked to the end of the bar where a section of it was cut so she could lift it up or pull it down. She pulled the section down behind her, as she went to the sink and washed her hands. After drying her hands, she grabbed a bottle of scotch and proceeded to pour the drink.

"Make that a double, would you please?" Aquarius asked the barmaid.

"Sure, why not?" the barmaid responded. "Do you want a glass with your beer?"

"Yes, unless you have a glass slipper that I can drink from."

The woman grinned and nodded her head, indicating 'no'. The barmaid brought Aquarius his drinks.

"Where's your drink?" Aquarius asked the barmaid?

"I drink champagne, eight dollars a bottle," she replied.

"Again, I ask you, where's your drink?"

She smiled and turned to the beer case and pulled out a pint size bottle of champagne and opened it in front of him and said, "Here's to you."

Aquarius picked up his drink, and they both clinked their glasses together and took a sip.

"Thank you, anything else?" the barmaid asked.

"You are quite welcome. What's your name?" Aquarius asked.

"Angel," she answered.

"Angel," he said as a group of four women walked into the bar and sat two seats down from him. "Give everyone in the bar a double of what they are drinking, plus the chaser to go along with it."

Angel stared at him.

"Oh, okay, I understand," Aquarius said with a grin. Aquarius reached into his suit jacket and pulls out two fifty-dollar bills. He handed both bills to Angel and she checked them with a black marker. "Okay?"

She smiled and walked away to serve the other customers their drinks. Each time Angel served someone, she would point to Aquarius and they thanked him for the setup. When Angel finished serving her customers, she added up the total and came down to where Aquarius was sitting and said, "Thirty-five even."

Aquarius looked at the money in front of him and nodded. Angel picked up a fifty, rung up the tab, and brought him his change. She placed the fifteen dollars on top of the fifty dollars on the bar in front of him, and said, "Thank you."

Aquarius replied, "You can thank me when I'm finished, otherwise you'll be thanking me for as long as I'm here and that's a bit too much, don't you think?" Aquarius asked with a sheepish grin on his face and a twinkle in his eyes.

Angel smiled and asked him his name.

"Aquarius," he responded.

"Water sign, huh?" Angel said smiling. "Do you want me to run a tab for you tonight for as long as you are here, Aquarius, so you won't be going back and forth into your pockets?"

"Looking out for me, Angel?"

Angel smiled and answered, "This place can get pretty rough at times, and I don't want to see you get taken advantage of."

"Thank you, Angel, for being my guardian angel. I'll tell you what." Aquarius pushed the fifty-dollar bill toward her. "That's yours, your tip, and you can put this on account for me," reaching into his left pants pocket and bringing out two one hundred-dollar bills. This way, I won't have to go into my pockets again as long as I'm sitting here." He looked at his watch, "It's seven o'clock, and I have three hours and fifteen minutes, deal?"

"Deal." Angel put her hand out and they both sealed the deal by shaking.

In about half an hour, the DJ starts playing. "It's Ladies' Night. Do you want to hear something now?"

"My quarter or yours?" Aquarius asked.

"The bar's," Angel answered. "What would you like to hear, Aquarius?"

"I wanna hear what you like."

"That's a bet." Angel walked down to the end of the bar and set up a tab for Aquarius. She then pulled two red-marked dollar bills out of the register and told one of the two original women to play three numbers she called out; the woman played the songs. The first record that played was *I Believe I Can Fly*. By the time the record finished, half the bar was full with women.

Aquarius saw all kinds of women. Good-looking, ugly, slim, skinny, fat, light, dark, tall, short, quiet, loud, young, middle-age, and seniors. Out of all these women, the only one he could see was Angel, and Angel knew it, because she felt the same way.

The second record came on, *Natural High*. While the record was playing, Angel so happened to take a glimpse down the bar to check on Aquarius while serving a customer and caught him about to pull off his wedding band. She excused herself. Angel walked down to where Aquarius was. She motioned for him to lean over; she wanted to say something to him.

Aquarius leaned over to hear what she had to say. "Listen," Angel whispered, "I might be outta line for saying this, but I'm going to say it anyway. Taking off your wedding ring won't change the fact that you are married. Some of these women in here aren't worth the price of a soda. Some of them are looking for some sugar daddy to take care of them and their six kids or their habit; then there are the few real women, good women who deserve a second chance at happiness with a good man. And, a few of both are looking at you. Now if you get lucky, that's fine, but there's not a woman in here that's good enough for you to take off your ring and that includes me, too. If you do not listen to anything else in your lifetime, you listen to this. No matter what you do, if you do it in front of your wife or behind her back, be a man about it. Don't be a little boy or a punk doing it, because that's all you'll ever be if you take off your wedding band. Don't be a bitch, there are enough of them in the black man's world as it is. Be the man I thought you were when you walked in here and still think you are."

Angel walked away, leaving Aquarius stunned for a few minutes in thought. He called her back.

"Yes, can I help you?" Angel asked, like she's disgusted.

"Can I have another drink?"

"Who wants it? Because I don't serve boys and I don't like punks. And, I'm a bitch myself."

Aquarius held up his left hand. The wedding band was back on his finger. Angel smiled and said, "That's better." She brought him his drink and his beer.

The third and last song came on, *You Are My Lady*. It eased the tension between them, as they both smiled.

Aquarius hadn't noticed the three big men sitting behind him in one of the booths. The biggest of the three came over and sat next to him. "Hey, bro', how ya doing?"

Aquarius turned his stool to the side and looked at the center of the man's chest, which was as broad as a small car engine block. Aquarius nodded his head right to left and moaned, "Oh shit."

"No, little brother, it's not like that. I know that you are strapped, but it's three pieces to your one. All I want you to do is to listen to me for a minute, that's all."

"Go on," Aquarius said.

"You see the barmaid, Angel? Well, let me tell you something, that's the first time she has smiled, grinned, or laughed in four years. Four years, bro', and you made it happen. You got her to do something that nobody around here could for four years. She likes you. Yeah, I know you're married, but still, if you two were to hook up anyway, just let me tell you this. If you ever hurt her, you won't be safe in hell. Enjoy your night. Don't worry about your back, because Angel is watching yours for you and we are watching hers." The big man returned to his companions back at the booth.

Aquarius took a sip of his drink and called Angel and ordered the three men a drink, a double. When Angel returned with the drinks on a small tray, she motioned for them to come and get them. Aquarius stopped her and said, "No, I'll take them over to the gentlemen."

"No, you don't want to do that," Angel said.

"Yes, I do." Aquarius took the tray, put his drink on it, and walked over to where the three well-dressed men were sitting. "Since I don't know who drinks what, you gents grab your drink," which they do. Aquarius began by saying to the man who came over to him. "If we do hook up and she hurts me, you three gorillas won't be safe in heaven; cheers, big bro'.

The three men stood up. Aquarius, who stood six feet and weighs in at 230 pounds of solid muscle, looked like a stop sign with teeth next to three telephone poles. All three gave Aquarius a long hard look, looking him straight in his eyes as he held up his glass into the air, not blinking an eye. Angel closed her eyes. Every pair of eyes in the bar was on Aquarius and the three men. The three men stared at Aquarius, then looked at each other. Then all four glasses clinked together. "To friendship," the biggest man said. "To friendship and, most of all, to Angel." Angel passed out.

•　　•　　•　　•

Scorpio was in the slightly crowded steak shop for about ten minutes before her order was taken. During the time she was waiting in line, three young teenagers came into the store—loud, using profanity and harassing some of the customers. A few would-be customers left out of fear. Some of the others had a look of sheer terror on their faces, although a few of them tried not to show it. Scorpio took one look at the punks and turned back around.

Scorpio, who was 5'9" and weighed 140 pounds, with green eyes and a chestnut complexion, is considered to be one of the nastier Correctors because of her fighting skills. She's also bi-sexual and really didn't care that much for the male gender one way or the other except for her husband), just simply ignored the young hoodlums.

A pretty teenage girl about sixteen, who was standing in line behind Scorpio, caught the eye of one the boys. "Hey, check out that fine piece of beef over there. Hey, watch this and learn something," the boy said as he walked over to the now shaking girl. "What's up?" the boy asked the girl. She said nothing. The other two boys were standing by the opened front door giggling. "What's your name, my soon-to-be-next lover?" the young boy asked. Again, the girl said nothing. The boy who seemed to be about seventeen, 5'8", about 130 pounds, with a high yellow complexion, and the loudest of the trio began to get irritated.

Meanwhile, Scorpio's order was taken and she stepped aside and the girl stepped up to the window and placed her order and she, too, stepped aside. The girl stood next to Scorpio, who could visibly see that the young girl was truly scared. Scorpio leaned over to the young girl and whispered into her ear. "Don't be afraid, little sister, I got your back." The girl smiled.

The boy asked, "Who that, your momma?"

"My aunt," the girl answered.

"Hey, Auntie, can I take your niece out?" he asked Scorpio.

"No, I don't think so, she has a friend," Scorpio answered.

"You got a friend, huh? What can dude give you that I can't give you?" the boy asked the girl. The girl looked up at Scorpio.

"Go ahead; tell him. I won't tell your mother."

"A good lay," the girl answered.

The reply not only shocked Scorpio, but also caught her totally off guard. She held her hand to her mouth to muffle the sound of her laughter. Everyone who was in earshot and heard the girl's reply busted out loud in laughter.

"Bitch!" the boy yelled as he lunged at the girl.

Scorpio stepped in front of the girl and sent a ferocious, bone-shattering left cross to the boy's right cheek, which lifted him three inches off the ground backwards to the floor. The boy, reeling from the onslaught, realized that his cheekbone was broken when blood started gushing out of his mouth. He screamed at Scorpio and the girl, "You two bitches are dead!" as he and his friends ran out of the steakhouse, into the parking lot and into a waiting car. With the boy sticking his head out of the open front passenger window, spitting out blood, "Listen, sweetheart, whatever you do, do not leave this store, do you understand me? Do you?"

Scorpio shook the young quaking girl gently.

"Yes, but where are you going?"

"Outside," Scorpio answered.

"What? You can't go out there, they will kill you!" the girl screamed at Scorpio. "I won't let you," she said, as she grabbed Scorpio by the waist and locked her arms around her body.

Scorpio manages to pull the girl in front of her. "You see what they are doing? They are just sitting there, trying to decide whether to come in here or wait for one or both of us to come out, and chances are, they won't wait too long to decide. They are not waiting too long for the cops to show up, either. Here, take this," Scorpio took off her wedding band and her engagement ring and handed it to the crying girl. "Listen to me, do not give this to anyone but...," she whispered into the girl's ear. When she finished, she asked the girl, "Do you promise? Do you promise?"

"Yes! I promise, goddamn you!" the girl shouted.

"Don't you go out there, do you hear me? Don't you go out there," she instructed as the girl broke down crying. And, for the first time since she married Aquarius, she felt loved. "If I don't go out there, me, you, and maybe some of these people might get hurt or maybe even killed. I don't want that and I know you don't want it. Someone, please call 9-1-1."

The girl turned and yelled to no one in particular and when she turned back around, Scorpio was standing at the front of the store, next to the door. The girl started toward the door when Scorpio screamed, "Get down!" Scorpio reached around to the middle of her back under her jacket and pulled out her 9-mm Glock pistol, just as five men jumped out of the car they were sitting in. With MAC-10s and other assorted semi-automatic handguns poised, they started charging toward the store at Scorpio.

Scorpio ran away from the entrance of the steakhouse, as the first barrage of shots started flying. Scorpio was hit instantly. One bullet hit her in the right-upper breast. She reeled from the impact as she returned fire, hitting her first target twenty feet away. The boy was dead as he hit the ground with a bullet in his forehead. The second shot hit Scorpio in the lower abdomen, the force of the impact sending her to the ground. Feeling the hot sensation in her stomach, she felt her insides ripped open. She realized that it was all over for her. Managing to get to her feet, she was just in time to drop two more of her attackers, a man and another teenage boy. A man (the second of two) fleeing back to the car never made it as the back of his head exploded. Scorpio felt the burning sensation of the third and forth bullets. One bullet slammed into her left inner thigh, the other into the left side of her chest. Scorpio hit the ground, still holding the pistol, and waited for her attackers to come and finish the job, or for her pounding heart to stop beating. Blood started to trickle from the left corner of her mouth, as she heard the faint wailing of sirens in the near distance.

Thoughts of her life started passing through her mind. She thought about her marriage to Aquarius and all the good times that they have had before and during their time with the Correctors. She only wished she could have had the chance to meet the Centaur. A blood-curdling scream broke Scorpio's train of thought. It was coming from her young friend. She mustered enough strength to pull her pain-racked body up just enough to take aim and shouted, "Hey, ass-hole!" to the young boy who had started the end of her short young life.

The boy turned and looked down at the bullet-riddled body of Aunt Scorpio, and the look of sheer terror spread all over his young face, as he spotted the weapon in her hand, aimed at him. "See you in hell, kid," Scorpio said as she pulled the trigger.

The bullet hit the young boy in the groin. He dropped to his knees, and she heard him moan, "Oh, fuck me." The second round hit him in his heart. The boy hit the ground backwards as the third and final round hit him in the forehead.

It was over, over for her newfound friend and over for her. Scorpio no longer felt the pain and her vision was starting to fade. She heard the young girl screaming, "Oh, miss, I didn't mean for this to happen; I didn't mean to get you killed."

"Honey, my name is..." the girl bent down so she could hear Scorpio.

The girl smiled, "That's a pretty name," she said through tears. "My name is Bonita, Bonnie for short."

A man came running up to the pair and with a 9-mm Glock in hand, looked around to make sure that everything was clear. He kneeled down to Scorpio and looked in shock at the bullet-riddled body of the young woman, and said, "Sweetheart, help is on the way; hang in there, young lady," in a strong reassuring voice.

After hearing that voice, the young woman knew that God had not forsaken her. Scorpio knew everything was going to be alright. She looked up at the stranger, holding up her body gently in his strong hands, and said, "Hello, Centaur."

The man was taken aback as the woman said with a big smile on her face, "I'm Scorpio."

The man's face turned ashen, as if he was just told someone in his family had died.

"Pleased to meet you, sir," Scorpio said as she smiled and took a deep breath, exhaling for the last time. Scorpio died. She died knowing she accomplished two things: One, saving the life of an innocent child and at the same time getting rid of some what she called trash; and two, getting her wish—meeting the Centaur.

The man lowered the body of the woman and shed tears as he prayed over her lifeless body. Bonita, realizing that Scorpio was dead, picked up her head and back, and held her, crying. "Why, dear God; why do the good ones always have to leave first? Please answer me, God, please answer me."

•   •   •   •

By ten P.M. Taurus, Cancer, and Aries were back at their apartments. Taurus was working on last minute details for the first job of the thirteen days of carnage, which was planned for Friday night. Cancer was lying across her bed, miserable from eating too much at the Olive Branch Restaurant. Aries, just coming from the bathroom, sat down on the love seat in the living room, and picked up the remote control of the 52-inch television.

Cancer and Taurus both heard the scream at the same time. It was a scream of sheer pain, the kind of pain that has hurt and remorse. Cancer reached the apartment first with her 9-mm in her right hand, as she slowly pushed the apartment door open with her left. As she slowly pushed open the door, she spotted Aries sitting, staring at the television set. Cancer slowly entered.

Taurus, with his 9-mm in hand, slowly came in behind her. "What's going on?" Taurus asked Cancer.

"Don't know, yet," she answered.

Once inside the apartment, Cancer told Taurus to check out the rest of the apartment. Taurus slowly and cautiously searched the rest of the apartment. Satisfied everything was in place and in order, he returned to the living room, looked at Cancer, and hunches his shoulders in confusion.

"She's dead. She's dead," Aries moaned. "Those motherfuckers killed her. Those stinking, no good mother fuckers killed her. I swear I am going to kill every punk in this fucked-up city. So help me, you're dead, dead!" Aries yelled at the top of her lungs. "Every last one of you punk-ass bitches is dead!" Aries screamed, "I'm going to have a field day in this mother-fucking city. I'm going to kill every fucking one of them."

"Who? Who, baby; who is dead?" Cancer asked.

Aries turned her head around and looked up from the love seat at Cancer and Taurus and said, "They've killed the baby. They've killed our little girl."

"Scorpio?"

"Scorpio is dead."

"What?" bellowed Taurus.

Aries turned up the volume of the television. "For the benefit of those of you who are just joining our broadcast, we are just about one block south from the Mount Airy Pizza and Steakhouse, where just about one-half hour ago at eight-fifteen tonight, there was a deadly shoot-out in the parking lot of the pizza and steakhouse that has left six people dead—five young men and one young woman.

"According to witnesses and Philadelphia Police, a fight broke out between the dead woman and one of the dead men. According to witnesses, the woman was protecting a young teenage girl who was in the steakhouse when one of three teenage boys came in and started harassing the girl. When the woman intervened, punches started flying when the boy lunged at the girl. The trio ran out of the steakhouse to the parking lot and got into a waiting car, which just sat there waiting. Police theorize it was waiting for either the woman or the girl or for the both of them to come out of the steakhouse.

"Witnesses inside the steakhouse said the woman made the girl promise to her that she would not leave the steakhouse. The woman then walked over to the front door, pulled out a 9-mm (which police found at the scene), and walked out of the steakhouse. Witnesses said that's when all hell broke loose. Five men, including the one who started the fight, came charging out of the car, brandishing semi-automatic weapons of their own, firing off the first rounds. In the exchange of gunfire all six people were killed, with the woman killing the teenage boy who started the melee last, after he attempted to go inside the steakhouse after the teenage girl.

"Witnesses said the woman died last with the girl holding her head on her lap, crying, "Don't go, please, don't go. Oh God, please send her back." Paramedics had to sedate the girl when she refused to let police or paramedics near the woman's lifeless body. The teenager is reported to be in shock. Philadelphia Police, however, are very interested in what the woman whispered into the girl's ear before she died."

Aries turned the television off.

● ● ● ●

"It's been two weeks now, and Aquarius still hasn't said a word; nothing, and we have a job to do," Leo complained at the meeting.

Aries gave Leo a hard cold stare that made even him uneasy.

"What?" Leo asked Aries.

"Leo, fuck you, fuck the job, and fuck this fucked-up city! Those kids that killed Scorp, they were high on drugs and beer, and Scorp knew it."

"Then that's why she let them get the first shots off," Cancer surmised.

"That's right," Aries continued, hoping that some sense of realty would surface in their drug and beer polluted minds. "Those kids didn't kill Scorp; those drug-dealing and corner-store deli lowlifes killed Scorpio. I, for one, am not leaving the City of Philly until I bury some of those child-molesting sons–of-bitches, with or without your help. So, saying that, whoever is with me, let it be known now, or forever hold your peace."

"They may bury you in an unmarked grave, too, Aries," Taurus remarked.

"'T', mother made them, mother had them, mother fuck them. They can kiss my motherhood as they lower my black ass into that unmarked grave," Aries snapped.

"I'm with you, Aries," Aquarius said, walking into the meeting.

"Then, that's that; starting tonight, some of the corner drugstores and some of the corner delis are going down," Taurus said. "Any questions?" he asked.

"Just one," Leo said, looking at Aquarius. "This goes to Aquarius. What took you so long?" Everyone laughed.

The doorbell rang as the Correctors' meeting was just about to end. Everyone looked at each other, wondering who could be at their door. "Who the hell could that be?" Libra said, looking out the window past the black shades. She turned and looked at the group and said, "It's a little girl."

"I'll go," Capricorn said. A minute later Capricorn escorted Bonnie into the meeting room. Everyone looked on in shock, surprised at Capricorn's behavior. "It's for you, Aquarius."

"Me?" Aquarius asked, stunned.

"Mr. Aquarius," the teenager began, "my name is Bonnie. I'm the one who got Mrs. Sadie killed." Everyone looked at the young child in shock. "I am so sorry," Bonnie said, as she burst out into a heart-wrenching cry. She cried so hard, it upset and brought tears to all the Correctors. "She's dead because of me. Dead, saving me instead of herself. I'm sorry, I am so very, very sorry. Please don't hate me, please," the young girl pleaded.

Aquarius rushed over to the crying girl. "No! Baby, No! You are not the cause of Mrs. Sadie's death." And, for the very first time since the death of his wife, Aquarius broke down in tears.

It took fifteen minutes for the Correctors to calm down and compose both Bonnie and Aquarius. When the Correctors finally got Bonnie and Aquarius composed, Bonnie sat down among them and told the whole story.

After Bonnie finished, "Oh, my god, little girl; even I don't think I could've taken all that action."

Bonnie handed Scorpio's wedding and engagement rings to Aquarius. He thanked her and told her not to go anywhere; he'd be right back. Aquarius left the room.

In the meantime, Bonnie asked, "Which one is Mr. Taurus?"

"That's me," the Bull stood up.

"I took these from outta Mrs. Sadie's jacket pocket before the cops came. Mr. Centaur told me not to show them to anyone, and to make sure I gave them to you."

"Mr. Centaur?" the Bull said in shock. "You've met the Centaur?"

"Yes, he kept the cops from questioning me that night, handing the Bull six business cards, reading 'Scorpio'. He's nice," she added.

The whole room was quiet for about two minutes.

"Who is Mrs. Tonya?"

Everyone looked at Gemini 2. Bonnie looked at her and said, "Mr. Centaur told me to tell you that the girls are doing fine and he wants you to come and see them. He said that he will arrange everything and not to worry about a thing. Oh yeah, I almost forgot…," she continued, looking at the Bull. "He said to tell you that the pact is still intact, and no laws have been broken as of yet. He told me not to be afraid to come here. He said that from now on, I am under the protection of Soul and the Centaur, and you would make sure that I got back home alright."

"Well, he was right about that, honey," Leo said. "From now on, if you have a problem, we have a problem, got it?"

"Got it," Bonnie laughed.

Aquarius re-entered the room, and handed Bonnie a gold rope chain necklace with all twelve Zodiac signs in gold, plus his and Scorpio's wedding rings. "Now, sweetheart, we will always be together."

"Thank you," Bonnie said, as Aquarius helped her put on the necklace.

•   •   •   •

The mayor came under a lot of pressure from the city council to justify his actions for the huge cost in overtime, since there was no unusual crime activity in the city from civil rights organizations the last three weeks since PERT began, and, finally, the threat of a lawsuit against the city and the police department for undue harassment in the constant questioning of Bonita (Bonnie) Harrison. He announced at a press conference that as of the time of the press conference, he was disbanding PERT and the city and its citizens went back to normal status, as did the state government.

•   •   •   •

For the first time in four years, Derrick Jenkins had all four of his daughters together in one place at the same time. All five were sitting in one of the four dining halls at the Four Sisters Dinner Club and Lounge. Each dining hall was named after one of Derrick's daughters. At the present time, they were in Justina's Golden Nugget. The Golden Nugget (like the rest of them) was built to hold up to 250 people; Justina's hall was strictly for dinner parties only;

Tynisha's blue hall was for business functions only; Christina's Violet Hall was for cabarets only; and, Tracy's Jade Hall was for the daily club and lounge functions, such as oldies but goodies parties.

The interior was painted gold with black trim. The chairs, tables and the table lamps were painted in gold with black trim. The windows were gold nuggets, shaped and painted gold with black trim. The curtains were the same as the windows, shaped as a gold nugget painted gold with black trim, as was the carpet on the floor. The dining room tables were also shaped like a gold nugget, painted gold with black trim and the chairs had low backs with a smooth soft cushion for comfort and ease.

"Okay, Daddy, what gives?" Tynisha asked.

"What do you mean?" Derrick asked.

"I mean, Daddy, you have been very quiet since that shoot-out a few weeks ago."

"You sure have," Justina added.

"You have that it's-the-end-of-the-world look. The last time you looked like that, was when you thought that mom was killed," Tracy jumped in the conversation.

"Wishful thinking," injected Christina. "Why the hell did you have to bring her up anyway?" Christina asked Tracy with a cold look in her eyes that could have frozen hell.

"Look, don't start that crap again," Tracy warned her sister.

"Stop it!" Derrick told his girls.

"Yeah, I'll stop it alright. I'll stop as soon as I find that piece of shit and kill her."

Derrick slapped Christina's face. Christina looked on in horror and disbelief at her father as he told her, "I don't give a damn how you think or feel about your mother, don't you ever, ever talk about your mother in that manner again. Do you understand me, young lady?"

Christina looked at her father, rubbing her face while fighting hard to hold back the tears.

"Do you?" Derrick asked again.

"Yes! I hear you, but do I understand? No. I do understand this much, Daddy. I understand that the first chance I get I'm going to blow that bitch right off the face of this earth. Now, do you understand that, Daddy? Christina asked her father as she stood up and the tears she fought so hard to contain fell freely down her cheeks. Christina started walking toward the door of the hall. She stopped, turned, and looked at her father and said, "I love you, Daddy, but I don't understand why you still protect her."

Christina turned and walked to the door as Derrick asked her to wait. Christina turned and smiled at her father and said, "Why? So I can turn the other cheek? I don't think so, Daddy, It hurts too much." Christina walked out the door.

"Damn, damn, damn, damn, damn," Tracy said, as she looked at her father in disgust. "Come on, let's go get her before she hurts herself," Tracy said to Justina. Both women get up to go and talk to their older sister.

Justina stopped, turned, and asked Derrick, "Damn, Daddy, did you have to hit her so hard?"

Derrick felt a tingling in his chest. He looked and said nothing as the two disappeared out the door.

"Dad, you've got to tell them; you have to tell them before Crissy destroys herself with hatred or kills our mother. She will kill her and you know it, Daddy."

Derrick felt the sting again. "I will; I'll tell them tonight," he told his oldest daughter. The third sting hit and, rubbing his left arm, Derrick started to sweat. He grabbed his chest and falls to the floor.

Tynisha screamed, "Daddy!"

•   •   •   •

"Okay, everyone knows what section of the city they have and their escape route?" Taurus asked the Correctors. Everyone nodded 'yes'. Aquarius will be at the short wave radio; it's tuned to the police band. If he says M-Y-A, move your ass. I don't care what you are doing, drop it and get your asses out of the area. Okay, one more time, let's hear the area the teams hit," said Leo. "Alpha team...Pisces and Capricorn...hit Nicetown. Bravo team...Aries and Virgo...hit Brewerytown. Charlie team...Gemini twins hit Tioga. Delta team...Taurus and I...hit East Falls. Echo team...Cancer and Libra hit the Fairhill section. Remember, we make buys first, just to make sure we are hitting the right scum. Leave, come back, and close them down. Buy from enough corners to cover a five-block area. In that way, the cops will have a wide area to cover. That will tie them up long enough for you to get the hell out of the area. Leo, the delis?"

"Do we hit the delis?" Cancer asked.

"Yes, we use the incendiary bombs."

"And, the children that might be in the delis?" Aries asked.

"Show them your police badge and tell them to go home, or go to jail. Little bastards shouldn't be out that time of night anyway," Teresa concluded. "Try and hit the pushers and the buyers only."

"Do we leave anyone alive?" Tonya asked.

"Ask Scorp, Tonya, ask Scorp," Teresa said smiling.

Aquarius looked at Teresa with a glare in his eyes that would have melted an iceberg. Teresa busted out in laughter.

"It's four o'clock. Go and check your gear, then get some shut-eye; we leave at midnight," Taurus ordered.

It was twelve-twenty when Alpha team made their first buy. By one-fifteen, Echo team had made their last buy. At one-thirty, Aquarius gave the command, "Hit 'em." It was over in less than an hour. It was two-fifteen by the time the last team (Echo) got back to Corrector's headquarters. At two-thirty all of the Correctors were watching the in-coming news flashes.

"We all have the next two days off," Taurus said, as he said goodnight.

By five A.M. every channel in the tri-state area was reporting on the night of terror, the news media dubbed the 'early-morning attack on Philadelphia'. "As of the last update, forty-four people are confirmed dead. The ages of the dead start as young as nine years old to seventy-seven. The number hurt is between thirty-two, and fifty-five. Police and doctors from various hospitals are having a hard time keeping an exact figure because some of the injured are still dying. The damage caused by this morning's attacks is estimated at over six million dollars in lost business. It looks like the attacks were mainly focused on street corner drug dealers and their buyers, and corner delis that sell beer. One known drug dealer, who was found shot to death in the East Falls section, is said to have had two business calling cards stuffed in his mouth. Philadelphia Police would not comment on the cards when asked about them. Inside sources said the calling cards have the Zodiac signs Gemini 2 and Scorpio on them...."

Click. Derrick turned off the television set from the remote control he was holding in his left hand, free from the IV protruding from his right arm. Derrick had been hospitalized for two days and was scheduled to be released the next day. As of the present time, Derrick wasn't sure if he really wanted to go home, not after the deadly attack on his beloved city.

SOUL has broken the pact that had been in place without incident for the last twenty-five years. Now he must plan to fight, or his much-loved city will die. Derrick called the mayor for a meeting as soon as he gets out of the hospital. Derrick hopes and prays that it's not too late to save his city from further damage. He knows deep in his heart it's wishful thinking. He knows deep in his heart and soul that before this thing is over, more people will die. The big question is will he be one of them. He knows if you fight Soul, you fight to the death, yours or theirs. Derrick prays that his girls do not have to get mixed up in this mess.

●　　●　　●　　●

"Are you out of your mind?" Taurus screamed at Tonya, as he paced back and forth in the meeting room. "Tonya, we just killed almost fifty people and they are still dying each day and we left that many in hospitals. Hell no! He just might kill you on sight, no!"

"No, he won't, Taurus, just listen to me. What the Centaur and I had, you just don't throw it away; put it out of your mind, your heart, your soul...."

"Noo, we just pick your cold, lifeless ass up and ship it to your family, providing we are able to get to your body," injected Aries.

You can forget that meeting-with-your-kids shit. As of last night, that's out of the question. That mother must be beyond livid; I bet that he's so pissed, you can cook an egg on the top of his head. You wanna meet with him now, of all times? No! And, on top of that, the first thing that's going to happen when he sees you is he might have a heart attack. You betrayed him, Tonya, you almost killed him. But what makes things even worse, you broke his heart when you put that bullet in his chest. The look on his face could have made Satan cry. All because of that slut you call a sister. I, for one, would've let the whore get what was coming to her."

"He was going to kill her, and you know that, Aries."

"Bullshit, all the Centaur was doing was giving her the ass kicking that your parents should've given that sex-craving, alcoholic bitch years ago. He never would've had to kill those three thugs in that alley if your sister hadn't gotten horny drunk and went out looking for some dick. Hell, if it wasn't for the Centaur saving her pitiful ass, she might have been one of those women you read about in the morning newspaper while drinking coffee, "Prostitute Found Dead in an Alley in Downtown LA." And, how do you show your gratitude? Because he started kicking her pitiful ass, you put a bullet in his chest, two inches above his heart."

"He was killing her, Aries, and you know it!" screamed Tonya, with tears in her eyes.

"You're a lying ass, Tonya. You were getting even, that's why he left you and took the kids to Philly with him. That's why your ass is divorced. You were getting even with him for fucking your sister. He was drunk, Tonya, drunk! And you and that slut are identical twins…identical. She was the one that came into your room in the dark and seduced him. If I were you, I would've kicked her black ass myself. He loved you, Tonya. He loved you and because of that blood-is-thicker-than-water bullshit you almost killed him. Sometimes even blood runs thin, Tonya."

"When we get back to LA one of us is going to die," Teresa warned Aries.

"Why wait, bitch? Let's do this now." Aries stood up out of her chair.

"Let's go," Teresa said, jumping up from the loveseat she was sitting on.

"Enough!" Leo shouted. "You three can settle your personal problems back in LA."

"Listen, we should wait and give the Centaur a reason to want a meeting," Libra interrupted, standing between Aries and Teresa.

"Sit down or I'll kick the both of your asses," Libra warned the two women, smiling. Both women sit down. "Otherwise, walking into his club the way you want may suggest an act of hostility."

"Libra's right," Taurus said. "With a set meeting, tensions won't be so high. Smart, Libra, smart. You don't say much, but when you do, it always makes sense. Tonight, we hit the oil refinery. Pisces, you and Cap are on for tonight."

"Let's light up the sky," Capricorn said smiling.

"Tonya," Taurus said in a stern and firm deep voice. "You are not to go anywhere near the Centaur or your children, do you read me?"

"Yes, I read you," Tonya said, pushing her way out of the meeting.

"Keep an eye on your sister, Teresa," Leo ordered. "This meeting is over."

"Shit isn't over for you and me," Teresa told Aries.

"Kiss my ass, whore," Aries responded.

"Kick your ass," Teresa grinned.

•　　•　　•　　•

"Hi, Daddy," Tracy said, as she walked into Derrick's private room at Walnut Hall Hospital.

"Hey, my baby girl," he responded.

"Dad-Dad, what's up Dude?" Tynisha asked, coming behind Tracy.

"Hi, Tiny," Derrick answered.

"Hey, hey, poppa bear; steal any pic-a-nic baskets lately?" Justina greeted her father.

"Hi, 'J'," Derrick grinned. "Where is Crissy?" he asked.

"Outside. She's waiting for us in the lounge," Tracy answered.

"Why didn't she come in with you?"

"Because she's acting like a fool. She thinks she is the reason for you having that heart attack," Justina replied.

"That's not possible, 'cause I didn't have a heart attack, it was a mild case of heartburn, you know, gas."

Tracy grinned, took two fingers, lifted up her nose, and sniffed. "You smell it?" she asked her sisters.

Justina answered, "Yeah, I smell it," grinning. "You smell it, Tiny?" Justina asked.

"Oh yeah, I smell it. Did you bring any shovels?" Tynisha asked, grinning.

"Shovels wouldn't help in this case."

"Why not?" Christina asked.

"Dad's been here two days; it's piled up too high."

Derrick broke out in a great big grin as he threw his pillows at his daughters and started laughing.

After sitting and talking for one hour, the three women said so long to their father and walked out of the room. After about five minutes of prodding, Christina is pushed into the room. "Hello, Dad," she said, as she burst into tears. "I'm sorry, Daddy."

"You are sorry? No, baby, I am the one who is sorry. I lost my temper and slapped you."

"Yeah, you did, Daddy, and I deserved it, too. I won't talk about her and I won't even think about her, ever again."

"That's not what I want you to do, baby. There are a lot of things that you don't know about your mother. When I get out of here, I...no, we will all sit down and I will tell you now. It will give you a different outlook in her favor. So, how is my headstrong little girl?"

"Well, Daddy, you can call me 'Cherry Cheek' for right now," pointing to the right side of her face. "I love you, Daddy."

"I love you, too, 'Cherry'." Christina laughed. "Are your sisters still here?"

"Yes, they're waiting for me in the waiting room."

"Tell them to come in, we've got to talk."

Christina walked to the door of the waiting room and motioned for her sisters to come back into their father's room. After the women came back, they all sat around their father's bed.

"Do not say anything until I am finished," Derrick said. They all agree. Derrick takes a deep breath and exhaled. He began, "About thirty-five years ago, a few friends and I started a club called 'Soul'. In the beginning, it was a social club—teenage bullshit—we had dances, gave parties for the younger kids in the neighborhood, and looked out for the seniors. We had social functions for ourselves. We had a lot of fun. Well, it came to an end for me when I went into the Army. When I came home on leave, people started telling me that the club had changed. I was told that they didn't do the things that they used to do—they were more private, stayed to themselves, more business-like. So, I went to see for myself. I was shocked. The membership had grown, now there were women, and they were in a business. I asked what kind of business...exterminating. 'Exterminating what?' I asked. They laughed, told me when my tour of duty was over—they knew I was good—then that's when they would fill me in. I was home for thirty days. In the time I was home, I met your mother."

Everyone looks at Christina. "What? I'm cool," she said, feeling her cheek. "Go on, Daddy," she told her father.

"In the little time I had home, we got tight. For twenty days, your mother and I were together. I met your grandparents, your aunts, and your uncle. We couldn't be separated. When I asked your mother what was going on, what kind of exterminating, she told me I would find out in due time. I gave your mother my address when I was going back to duty.

"The third year I was in the service, I was transferred to Germany. Your mother surprised me and came to Germany to visit me; she left Germany after eighteen months and as Mrs. Jenkins. After we were married, that's when she told me that the Club Soul was now in the business of exterminating people. Yes, they were now paid assassins. I asked her how she could be a part of such a thing. She said she wasn't. She was there to break it up, protect her sister, and pull her out. That's when she showed me her ID badge. Your mother is FBI and the rest of the story you know."

Christina, Justina, and Tracy were stunned. They sat around their father in pure shock. The three women then looked at their sister Tynisha.

Christina said, "You knew…you knew, goddammit, you knew. How could you, Tiny? How could you let me hate my mother for all these years and not tell me? How could you, Tiny? How could you?" Christina broke down crying.

"Believe me; I wanted to tell you years ago."

"It's not her fault, it's mine," said Derrick. "Your mother made me promise not to tell you. She wanted to tell you herself. Now that Soul has broken the pact, they know that I will be coming after them."

"That's not exactly true, Daddy. By you going after them, and they are well aware that you will be, they will be gunning for you first," Christina spoke up. "And, by them coming after you, that means they will be coming after us, too, knowing we are not going to just stand by and let a bunch of lunatics kill our father," interjected Justina.

"Your mother won't allow that to happen."

"Hell, Daddy," that means she's in trouble, too," Tracy said.

"Does the mayor know all of this?" Tynisha asked.

"No, but we have a meeting after I get out of here."

"I still don't understand something," Christina said. "What does the FBI have to say about all of this? Why haven't they pulled her out after all of this time, or arrested the whole damn bunch?" Christina asked testily.

"For one, if they tried to pull your mother out, she wouldn't leave without your aunt. Secondly, if your mother did manage to pull your aunt out, Soul would most likely hunt them down and kill the both of them. Let me tell you kids something," Derrick told the four sisters. "Your aunt has gotten good at what she does, and that makes her dangerous. But, what makes her even more dangerous, she likes what she does. Your mother fears one thing…"

"And that is, Daddy?" Tynisha asked.

"Your mother fears that if Soul comes after me or any one of you, she might have to kill her own sister. Remember one very important thing. Your mother and your aunt are identical twins. They have the same height, nearly the same weight and same color complexion. Really, the only way you can tell them apart is to look into their eyes."

"What's up with their eyes, Daddy?" Tracy asked with a curious look in her own eyes.

"Your aunt's left eye has a small star in the upper left-hand corner. It's a birthmark, and if that star comes into direct contact with light, it shines. The light temporally blinds her. That's why she wears special custom-made contact lens."

"What color are Mom's eyes?" Christina asked her father.

Derrick smiled, "Look in the mirror, honey, look in the mirror," he responded.

Christina smiled, grabbed and hugged her father, and softly cried. "I'm going on unpaid leave of…"

"No!" Derrick cut Justina off. "Go about your normal daily activity. Don't let them know that you are aware of their presence. They already know I'm aware of their presence."

"How's that?" Justina asked.

"I told them."

"You what?" Christina asked.

"The night of the shootout, the woman who was killed called me by name. How she knew who I am is beyond me. She introduced herself before she died. Her name was Scorpio. She gave that little girl she was protecting her engagement and wedding rings. She also gave her six calling cards, and told her whom to give them to before she died. I just want all of you to be careful, very careful. This is my fight and my fight only."

"Not anymore, my father," Christina interrupted. "Those bastards have my mother, and I'll be damned if I don't get her back. Hell or high water, I'm freeing my mother. They want a fight…they got one hell of a fight coming," Justina said.

"You got that right, do or die," Tynisha added.

"The shit is on," Tracy concluded in a battle tone.

Derrick smiled because he knew there was nothing that he could say or do to stop his daughters. The four sisters were pissed.

•   •   •   •

It was eleven-forty by the time Pisces and Capricorn finished setting the charges on the tanks at the oil refinery. They set eight C-4 charges, one at every other storage tank. One tank would explode every thirty seconds. It would be over in four minutes. Capricorn signaled to Pisces that he was finished setting his charges. Pisces signaled back, indicating that he, too, was finished. The two met at the hole in the chain link fence they made to gain access.

"What about the two guards we left?" Pisces asked.

"Don't worry about them; they are with their higher power or their lower power, whichever. Who gives a shit? Let's go, I'm hungry," Capricorn smiled.

"There's a deli about two miles down the road from here; we can grab a bite, make the call, and watch the fireworks from there," Pisces said. Pisces drove down the lonely stretch of highway doing about sixty- five miles an hour. When Pisces passed an old torn billboard hanging half down on its post, he looked into the rear view mirror. Pisces frowned and stated to Capricorn, "We've got company," spotting the flashing red and blue lights.

"Shit," Capricorn responded.

Pisces continued driving at the present speed. After driving a few minutes, going down the road, they heard the policewoman's demand for the driver to pull over to the right-hand shoulder over the cruiser's PA system.

"Damn," mumbled Pisces, as he pulled over as instructed.

Rosemore Blvd. was a long strip of road alongside of the oil refinery, stretching three miles long. The road was dark traveling east, and had very little light traveling west. Pisces and Capricorn were traveling east. On Pisces' side of the road, all you could see was the dozens of huge round tanks containing raw oil. On four of the tanks was painted the logos of the four major sport clubs the city had to offer—a baseball, a basketball, a hockey puck, and a football.

On the passengers' side, Capricorn observed the close cropped housing area. The housing area was known as the Rosemore Blvd. Projects. A closed-in, low-income complex, which was dully lit and strewn about with abandoned cars, all of which were stolen and stripped or left to be reported to have been stolen. Trash dumpsters, some filled to capacity, others overflowing, with debris surrounding the canisters like Indians surrounding a fort, just waiting for the order to attack. A chain link fence enclosed the entire complex, except for the opening. In some areas, the fence stood tall, straight, and shiny from the silver it was painted, while other areas were bent over, cut open, and rusted.

After Pisces pulled over to the side of the road, the pair watched as the police car pulled about twenty yards behind them, and waited for the officer to approach them. The waiting game began. After five minutes of waiting, Capricorn wondered out loud, "What's taking that cop so long?"

"She's checking the plates," Pisces answered.

"Is she alone?" Pisces asked.

"Yeah, why?"

"I'm getting ready to give that bitch a driving lesson."

"No!" Capricorn said in a whisper. "We've got less than ten minutes," looking at his watch, "to get out of this area and we can do it if you keep your cool."

"Fuck cool, cold is what I'm worried about. If that chick finds our equipment in this car and the rest of the C-4 in the trunk, that my friend is cold, and that's not cool."

"Point taken, let's get out of here."

"Oh shit, it's too late."

"What?" Capricorn asked.

Pisces pointed to an offset road to his right. Capricorn looked in horror, as he watched the six police cars approaching them.

"Turn on the police band," Capricorn said.

"No time, let's get the hell outta here." Pisces started the car and drove down the road, coming to a sudden stop after driving one hundred yards.

"Now what?" Capricorn asked.

"Look down the road and see, Cap."

Capricorn looked and saw the road and the four police cruisers blocking their path.

"We go back the way we came," Pisces mumbled as he spun the car around and headed back toward the rigged oil tanks. "Look," Pisces grinned, as he saw the lone police cruiser blocking the road with the police officer aiming a double barrel shotgun their way. Pisces stopped short about thirty yards from the policewoman.

"Shut off the vehicle and lock your hands behind your heads; do not step out of the vehicle," the officer demanded.

Pisces, looking at his watch, looked at Capricorn and said, "Listen, as it looks and the way I see it, we have three options. One, we can surrender and live long enough for them to inject our asses; two, we can make a stand and die right here; or three, we can make a run for it and make it back to the hot tanks, and take half or all of those motherfuckers with us. It's up to you, Cap," Pisces grinned.

"I repeat, shut the engine off and lock your hands behind your heads; do not get out of the vehicle, now!" the officer again demanded.

"Well, Pi, do we have tickets to the dead pig's ball?"

"What the hell do we need tickets for? It's more fun to crash a party," Pisces smirked as he floored the gas pedal. The car screamed as it raced toward the officer.

The police officer stepped out of the cruiser, aimed the shotgun toward the oncoming car, and fired. Capricorn, seeing the officer aiming the shotgun in his direction, ducked down underneath the dashboard. He lifted his head after the first volley passed through the windshield, just in time to catch the second volley of shotgun pellets. The red-hot pellets ripped into Capricorn's face, head, and neck. Capricorn slumped backwards in the seat with his head hanging over the headrest. Pisces, knowing that his best and truly his only friend was dead, bolted past the policewoman, grinning, "Come and get me, bitch."

The officer jumped back into her cruiser and gave chase, with four other police cruisers behind her. Pisces looked at his watch, eleven fifty-seven. He thought that was enough time to get back to the rigged tanks and wait for his guests. At eleven fifty-eight, Pisces came to a stop in between the second and third rigged tanks. Pisces wiped some of Capricorn's blood and bone fragments from the right of his face. Pisces looked at his fallen friend and said, "Don't worry about it, buddy, I'll be joining you real soon.

Guess what, Cap? I'm taking that bitch piece of shit and some of her friends with me." Pisces noticed three police cruisers come to a stop about twenty yards ahead of him, and the policewoman and the four cruisers thirty yards behind him. Pisces looked at Capricorn for the last time, smiled, and said, "I'm coming, my friend. Do me a favor and tell Satan's wife to set extra plates, I'm bringing company."

The next second there was a flash, a huge ball of bright orange and red, and then the sound. The impact of the blast sent the car Pisces and Capricorn were huddled two hundred yards across the road, smashing into and disintegrating a house. The five unsuspecting occupants of the two-story dwelling never knew what hit them. The five police cruisers that were behind Pisces and Capricorn were blown into the air, smashing into one another, bursting into flames while airborne. The nine officers never had a chance. The second, third, and fourth explosions made short work of the remaining three police cruisers blocking Pisces and Capricorn's exit. The eight officers died instantaneously from heat asphyxiation before burning up, while still sitting in their cruisers. Lucky for the arriving firefighters, police officers, and the remaining three-fourths of Rosemore Blvd. Projects, the remaining four tanks did not explode. Due to Capricorn's haste in setting the timers on the fuses, he set them to go off in thirty hours, instead of thirty seconds. It took firefighters thirteen hours to bring the inferno under control, with the loss of three of their own.

•　　•　　•　　•

Tracy Jenkins' funeral was the first of the twenty police and firefighter's services to be held in the city in the first week following the oil refinery holocaust. Seven thousand police and firefighters from all over the country attended the services. Security was tight; the Secret Service and other federal, state, and local law enforcement agencies were present, since the President of the United States was attending all the funeral services. Some you could identify, and some you couldn't. The president proclaimed thirty days of mourning, honoring the fallen police and firefighters. Four of the services were en masse, because all that was left of the bodies was ashes and could not be separated. The City of Philadelphia, State of Pennsylvania, the country, and some parts of the world were in complete shock and mystified. How and why could something like this happen?

What could justify this senseless act of genocide? The country and the citizens of Philadelphia were angry and the Correctors knew it.

Neither Derrick, nor his remaining three daughters or Debra Carver-Jenkins shed a teardrop at his baby girl and their baby sister's funeral, they were too angry. They were too angry and blinded with fury to notice Tonya Jenkins at the service. Tonya watched as the honor guard handed the neatly folded flag to her ex-husband. It was too much for her when her eldest daughter, dressed in her class blue uniform, pressed the toggle switch to lower her beloved baby girl's casket into the ground.

Tonya screamed and fell to the ground, passing out. Derrick, recognizing the scream, rushed past some of the attendees and over to his ex-wife. Without saying a word to anyone except 'pardon' or 'excuse me', Derrick reached Tonya and gently picked her up and carried her to a waiting limousine.

Tynisha, Christina, Justina, and Debra, watching the scene, waited until they threw their rose on their sister's casket before joining their father. Derrick never noticed Cancer mixed among the crowd of mourners watching the events unfold. Cancer had the look of mixed satisfaction and deep, dire concern on her face as she left the service. As Cancer sat in her car, she smiled and said to herself, *I'm glad someone can go home since I can't. I'm glad it worked out like this, now I won't feel too bad when I kill the bitch.* Cancer laughed out loud as she pulled off.

No one said anything on the way back to the family home, located in the Roxborough section of the city. Debra Carver-Jenkins asked to be dropped off at her apartment. "Deb, the car will be back for you in three hours."

"Thanks, Fam," Debra said, "see you then," as she walked down the pathway to her apartment building.

Christina just looked at the woman with her head lying on her father's lap. You could visibly notice the teardrops falling down and drying on Tynisha's face as she just sat, staring at the woman. Uncertain whether to be happy or to be concerned, Justina and her sisters knew instantly who the woman was as soon as their father picked her up. The question is was she here to stay or will she or one of her sisters will have to eventually kill their own mother? A thought neither she nor her sisters even wanted to think about.

Derrick could see and sense the happiness, the apprehension, the reluctance, and the gratification; the questions written all over his daughters' faces.

He decided to let nature take its own course of action and see then what the final outcome would be. Time and only time would tell.

•   •   •   •

"I don't believe this! This shit is not happening. It's not real; it can't be real." Aries was ranting as she walked back and forth at the Correctors' meeting. "All we had to do is to come here, kill a man—one man—and leave. One man, mind you. But, noo... What do we do? We start off by losing our baby girl in a senseless gunfight."

"Aries, don't."

"Shut up!" Aries snapped at Taurus. "This is my nervous breakdown and I can have it if I want to. And, as I was saying," Aries continued, as the remaining Correctors looked on in silence. "We kill forty, forty-five people—men, women, and some children. Children, for Christ's sake, while blowing up city street drug corners. We blow up an oil refinery, which still doesn't make any sense to me. But, this is the kicker; in the process, we manage to kill our second leader's daughter. And, to make matters worse, it's his baby girl. Capricorn and Pisces are dead. The Centaur has Tonya and we don't have the slightest idea where Aquarius is. Hell, he hasn't been the same since Scorpio's death. But, this is the grand prize. We have the president of the strongest country in the fucking world pissed off at us. He's got every federal law enforcement agency he commands after us. The goddamn mob is on our shit. Every fucking cop on the entire East Coast wants bragging rights for killing, one, two, or all of us. No telling what the Centaur has in store for us. Hell, I'm not even worried about him as much as I am his daughters. They have to be some pissed off, mad bitches." Aries stopped and directed her attention to Cancer. And, as far as you, Cancer, no matter how or what you feel about Tonya, girl, she is going to kill you. No ifs, ands, or buts about it, you are one dead sister. For the love of God, Taurus, we've killed children, little children. Man, just exactly what the hell are we doing? Please, somebody tell me what the hell we are doing?" Aries sat down and broke out in a hearty cry.

"Man, we have got to get her to a doctor," Libra stated to Taurus.

"No! We can't do that. We first have to get out of here, or we all are going to need a doctor," Taurus responded. "She'll be alright; she's just hurt right now, just like the rest of us are. Once we get out of here and get some rest; we'll all be fine…start packing."

"Where are we going?" Virgo asked.

"My mother once told me, 'It's a poor rat with only one hole,'" Leo responded, laughing, "let's move it."

•　　•　　•　　•

The Jenkins family, including Tonya, was in the den of their Roxborough home about to talk when the doorbell rang. The den was larger than a regular-sized den. It had two love seats, sofa, five La-Z-Boy chairs, and twelve paintings of different time periods surrounding the den, from the time of Jesus Christ to modern day. A wall clock with the pictures of his girls…Tonya, Debra, and himself in the center. The floor was covered with a deep shag carpet; like all the furniture, it's chocolate in color, and there's a glass and marble coffee table in the center of the furniture with an intercom system sitting on it. The den was brightly lit with round and oblong floodlights with two brown ceiling fans in the center of the surrounding lights.

Rosa, the head maid, answered the door. A minute later, Debra Carver-Jenkins entered the den. Christina broke out with a big grin. "Hey, girl," Christina said.

"What's up, Fam?" Debra asked.

Tonya looked uncomfortable.

"Mom, this is my best friend and our adopted sister, Debra Carver-Jenkins. Deb, this is our mother, Tonya Jenkins."

Tonya stood up from the easy chair she was sitting in and hugged Debra, who had walked over to her.

"Oh shit! You do have a mother; I thought you bitches were products of a test tube."

Derrick burst out in loud laughter. Tonya liked Debra instantly.

"We were about to have some lunch and a sit down; join us?" Derrick asked.

"Hey, Dad, like you're gonna put me out?"

"Oh, like I can't?"

"Hey! Will somebody please remind Pops that I am a deranged cop and I am carrying?"

Tonya looked at Debra and held her stomach as light tears start rolling down her cheeks, while she tried to hold in her laughter.

Debra looked at Tonya and said, "Oh hell, yeah, you all related. I just hope you don't cry as much as my Crissy. That's the cryin'est mother I've ever seen in my life."

Tonya screamed from the cramps in her stomach from laughing so hard.

Debra, looking at Tonya, said, "The whole damn family is crazy." Everyone laughed.

After lunch, Rosa took their trays, cleaned up, and asked, "Is there anything else?"

Derrick answered, "No, Rosa; that will be all, thank you."

"You're welcome," Rosa replied and left.

Christina asks her mother, "Mom, who or what is Soul, and why are they here?"

"Crissy, there is no such thing as Soul; they are the Correctors. They are here to kill Waters."

"Waters, the mayoral candidate? But why?" Justina asked.

"Wait a damn minute," Derrick interrupted. That's the name Tracy mentioned, who rented out the two triplexes; I thought that they were a big company or something like that."

"Mrs. Jenkins," Debra began to speak.

"Mom," interjected Tonya.

Debra smiled. "Mom, why do the Correctors want to kill Waters?"

"The people who hired us put a contract out on him. The contract is worth twenty-six million dollars. They paid us thirteen million in advance, the other thirteen when the contract is completed. They do not want Waters to get into office. If he does, it will mess up their plans. And if we don't kill Waters, they will have another outfit kill Waters and us, too. Derrick, they changed the club name after you left the West Coast. Somehow, someway we've got to stop them."

Derrick turned to Debra and said, "Deb, I don't want you to get mixed up in this mess. It might get very dangerous and..."

"And nothing!" Debra snapped, breaking into Derrick's sentence. "Dad, don't come at me with that someone-might-get-hurt-or-killed or this-is-a-family-matter bullshit. Dad, you answer me one thing. Am I a part of this family?"

"Yes, of course, you are. What kind of a damn fool question is that?"

"Am I your daughter?"

"Yes," Derrick replied.

Debra turned to Tynisha, Christina, and Justina and asked, "Am I your sister and are you my sisters?" The three women nodded their heads in agreement.

She then turned to Tonya, "Am I not your new daughter and you my new mother?"

"Yes," Tonya answered.

"Then, as your sister and as your daughter, I have every right to be here. I have every right to take part in bringing those lowlifes in, or killing them, whichever comes first. They can make it easy or they can make it hard. Frankly, I hope to God they make it hard. They've killed my fellow officers, killed fire-fighters, killed civilians, and the worst of all, they killed my baby sister. I am 5'8", 160 pounds of nasty, mad, black bitch. They are going down, Fam; they are going down. If I can't help you with your blessing, then I'll do it without. Any questions?" Debra asked as she wiped tears from her face.

Looking at Debra in total disbelieve, no one answered. "Good," Debra said, "now let's get down to business."

Tonya stood and took the floor. "Okay, everyone, listen and listen well; these are the members. One, Taurus the Bull, the leader; he's as strong as a bull, too. I once saw him grab two men in headlocks and broke both their necks at the same time. He's 6'5", 230 pounds; eyes black as coal; black hair, cut short; skin black as ebony; sweet, beautiful smile and gentle as a lamb, that is, until you make him mad, then he's dangerous, and I do mean very dangerous. He's fifty and single, with no children.

Two is Leo the Lion, second in command. He's nasty, cunning, and power hungry. Leo will kill at will. If anyone gets in his way, they are good as dead. He stands at 6'2" and goes around 300 pounds, reddish-brown hair in a small 'fro, brown eyes, and walnut-colored skin, smooth as a baby's ass. He's forty-nine and single, with no children.

Three is Aquarius, the water bearer, sergeant at arms. He's cool under pressure, a keen sense of direction, and very alert; he can hear a rat piss on cotton half a block away. He can't stand loud noises; it hurts and knocks his sense of balance off. Any of you who take him on, have a whistle with you, it may save your life. At times very playful, will only hurt or kill if necessary; very soft spoken, never raises his voice, even when killing. He's 6' and 230 pounds of solid muscle; very strong, light walnut eyes, light dirty brown hair, and light-skinned. He was married; no children, as she couldn't have them. He was devoted to his wife. He may have talked lots of shit to other women, but he would never betray his wife. He's thirty-one.

Four, Virgo the Virgin, the social ambassador. Happy go lucky, nothing seems to bother him; very shy, always smiling and that makes him very dangerous. Ex-pro boxer, he once killed a man in the ring, and after that, he quit. Very handsome and a very good con artist; he could con you out of your underwear while you were still wearing them. He's 5'9", 170 pounds; dark brown hair and brown eyes; and pecan-colored skin. Single, never married, and no children. He's twenty-nine.

Five is Libra the Scales, the treasurer; 5'11" and 160 pounds. She's quiet, polite, and very sweet, and I do have to admit she's pretty. She's the strongest of the women. She can be cold blooded, at times, and I do mean cold-blooded. She punched a woman she was fighting in her chest and the woman died two weeks later. When she says stop, you stop or you might get hurt or die. She has strawberry ice cream colored skin, red hair, and she is the only black woman I've seen in my life with natural blue eyes. Never married, no children, no family ties, and she's thirty-six.

Six is Cancer the Crab, business officer. She is the most beautiful black woman I've ever come into contact with in my life. She is also, by far, the coldest bitch on the planet. This sister could jump into an active volcano and freeze the lava. She would kill her own mother if she had a contract for her. She's 5'11" and 200 pounds. She has long, wavy, jet-black hair that comes to her waist, which she mostly keeps in braids; black eyes, and her skin is ebony brown and as smooth as silk. She is now the youngest member of the group. She's twenty-six, with four brothers and three sisters. She's the oldest and sends two-thirds of her pay back to her mother in the West Indies. With the help of Leo and Libra, they killed her father, made it look like a mugging. Her little sister had told her that their father was beating up their mother and spending the money she was sending her on his whores.

Seven is Aries the Ram, a regular member. I don't know what to say about this woman. She's cute as a button and very bubbly. The girl is wacky, she loves to have fun. She and Virgo are meant for each other. She's 5'7" and 130 pounds; has brown hair, loves her Jeri-curls, cut short; brown eyes; and light brown skin with freckles. She is the fastest of everyone, the girl can move. She is also the deadliest shot I've ever seen. We had a job and our target was at a football game. It was a Super Bowl. Our target was at one goal post and she was at the other, and she still managed to take him out at half time, and sat there and finished watching the game. The only time that girl gets serious is when we have a job to do. Other than that, she'll pull a prank on you in a minute, and nobody gets mad. Honestly we can't get mad; we all know how she is.

Eighth and last, but not least, Gemini the Twin, public relations. Teresa is the first born of twins by three minutes. She is 5'9" and 150 pounds. She has light brown hair, lemon core colored skin, and light brown eyes. She is evil, cunning, and she is slick as oil; knows how to use a knife and keeps several of them on her. Knows how to use a gun. She's not as good as Aries, but good enough. Put it like this, if Aries is an expert, then Teresa is a sharpshooter. She loves sex, and loves to get drunk. If she can't get drunk while drinking, she won't drink. Teresa will fight you, drunk or sober. It takes a lot to make her mad, but when she is, she has the nastiest temper God gave to any human being. She will kill you. Her specialty is breaking necks. She does it better than Taurus. Teresa is forty-four."

"Well damn, Mom, you just gave an exact description of yourself, I mean except for the bad things," Debra exclaimed.

"Debra," Tonya smiled and said, "Teresa is my twin sister."

Debra sat, stunned.

"Listen, girls, and listen good. If, and only if, you or we ever run into either of these women, remember this. They are good at hand-to-hand combat; all of them can fight. If you go one-on-one with any of them, you fight to kill. Believe me, you won't have any choice. And one other thing, they know that you girls have degrees in the martial arts. Derrick, they keep up-to-date records on you and the girls. They now have to change their plans. They know I will tell you everything. They will surely come after me now."

"Who do you think they will send, Mom," Christina asked.

"Aries or Cancer, or maybe both."

"What about Aunt Teresa?" Justina asked.

"No, they won't pit sister against sister; Taurus won't allow that." Tonya noticed her girls staring at her. "I know what you are thinking."

"Do you, Mom?" Christina asked.

"Yes, I do; you are wondering if I am your mother or if I am your aunt."

"Damn," Justina commented.

"Listen, girls, I don't blame you for feeling the way you do. I come back into your life like a bat out of hell. You are looking at me as the enemy; I was on the side of the people who killed your sister. But, you have to remember, that was my baby girl they killed. I warned them to keep my children out of this. They didn't heed my warning and I, with the help of you five, am going to kill them all. Debra, I too want them to make it the hard way. There are only two ways I can prove to you that I am your mother."

"Which are?" Christina asked with a frown on her face.

"Whoa, time out, wait just a damn minute. Somebody tell me what's going on? What did I miss? Debra asked, confused.

"It's like this, sis," Justina jumped in to answer her confused adopted sister. "Like Mom said, she and Aunt Teresa are twins; not only are they twins, but identical twins. But you see, Aunt Teresa was born with a birthmark..."

"So? Half the damn population of the country is, so what?"

Debra cut in. "Let me finish, would you? Aunt Teresa's birthmark is a star in the upper left-hand corner of her left eye. You see, if that star comes into direct contact with light, it temporarily blinds her, so she has to wear special custom made contact lens."

"Okay so all we have to do is to see if she is wearing contact lens. We just take an eyedropper and drop some water in her eye and see if it runs down her face," Debra suggested.

"Sounds stupid, but I'll go along," Tynisha said.

"Do we have an eyedropper here?" Justina asked.

"I'll ask Rosa for one," Derrick said.

"Yeah, and I already know the second way," Christina said in a hostile tone.

"Shut up, Crissy," Justina snapped.

"You shut up," Christina snapped back. "Look, Mom, I'll tell you what, you take both tests—one in front of us and the second, well, you know where you have to take the second one. You pass both and everything is cool."

"And, what if I pass one and fail the other?"

"Then I'll kill you myself," Christina answered in a cold tone of voice.

"Christina!" Derrick shouted.

"No, Dad, leave her alone," Tynisha protested.

"What if I don't take the test?" Tonya asked.

"Mom, then I'll kill you anyway," Christina answered testily.

"What will happen if I pass the first test and fail the second and your father tells you I passed?"

"Won't work, Mom," Christina answered impatiently. "Mom, Tracy taught us a trick. Her being the baby, she was always underneath Daddy, even when she got grown. It used to make me sick to my stomach. But, now today, I'm glad she did. She showed us how to tell when Daddy was hiding something from us. She showed us how to tell when Daddy was lying to protect us from something. We used to get over on him all the time, especially at Christmas time."

"Hell, we still do," Justina added.

Derrick smiled and said, "I let you think you were getting over."

"Yeah…yeah right, Daddy," Tynisha grinned.

"If Daddy was to try that, then I would just simply kill you both," Christina answered angrily.

"Oh shit, and these bitches are serious," Debra mumbled.

"Too damn serious for me," Derrick said in a shaky voice.

Damn, Debra thought to herself. *He may have a bad heart, but ain't a damn thing wrong with his hearing.*

Christina pressed a button on the intercom system. "Rosa, would you bring an eye or ear dropper and a small glass of water, and the menu for the day? Thank you."

"Right away, and you are welcome, Ms. Christina," Rosa replied.

In about two minutes, Rosa entered the den. Rosa, who is mixed, half Indian and half Mexican, stands 5'6" and weighs about 200 pounds. She has mixed silver and gray hair. She's sixty-one. She has been with Derrick and his girls since Tracy was six months old. She is very protective of all of them, including Debra. She has a second-degree black belt in Karate and Judo. She speaks English, Spanish, and Italian. "Do you mind my asking what you are going to do with the water and eyedropper, Mr. Jenkins?" Rosa asked.

"Well, Rosa, this might sound stupid but it's an identity test for Mrs. Jenkins."

"Oh, I see, but it's not necessary. I can tell you if she is Ms. Tonya or if she is Ms. Teresa."

Derrick was shocked as was everyone else, but Tonya was smiling.

"Mr. Jenkins," Rosa continued, "when you and Mrs. Tonya came home to visit a month before Ms. Tracy was born, you brought Ms. Teresa with you. Mrs. Jenkins told me her concerns about her sister. I saw through Ms. Teresa. I am sorry, Mrs. Jenkins."

"It's alright, Rosa."

"With Mrs. Jenkins permission, I gave her a tattoo on her right back. Then I told her two code names. Come here, girls, I will tell you the code names."

The four women went to Rosa and she whispered the two code names in their ears. "Ladies, remember one thing, please. If any one of you is confused, if you have your mother and your aunt together, you then ask your mother and your aunt the code words. Whoever answers right is your mother."

The four women squealed with joy.

"And, as far as the tattoo is concerned…"

Tonya lifted up the back of her blouse and revealed the tattoo, 'JENKINS 4 EVER'; the four women all smiled.

"I love you, Rosa," Tonya hugged Rosa.

"Love you, too, Mrs. Jenkins. Now, if there isn't anything else?"

"No, Rosa, there isn't…"

"Oh, yes there is," Derrick said. "Payroll will be adding twelve thousand dollars to your yearly salary."

"Thank-you, Mr. Jenkins, but that's not necessary," Rosa replied.

"May not be, Rosa, but it's a done deal."

Rosa smiled, and left the room, taking the water and the eyedropper with her.

"Okay, thanks to Rosa, we won't have to make total damn fools outta ourselves," Christina said. "Dad, Mom, we have decided that you two need some time together. Mom, you need to get the feel of your bedroom again and, Dad, you have to help her. You pass that test and I will be satisfied," Christina said.

"We'll call you at dinnertime," Justina added.

"If you two make a baby, make sure it's a boy," Tynisha snickered.

Yeah, right, those two old ass dinosaurs, please," Debra said laughing.

"Watch it, kid," Derrick said as he and Tonya walked up the stairs.

"Don't kill him, Mom; it's been a long time."

"How do you know?" Tonya asked Christina jokingly.

"Hell, Mom, he's twenty pounds overweight. When he comes back down, he'll be twenty pounds lighter and you'll be twenty pounds heavier."

All the girls started laughing.

"Very funny, smart ass," Derrick said laughing. "Damn kids are nuttier than a fruitcake."

"Your fault," Tonya said laughing, "they take after you."

"Right."

•   •   •   •

"Aquarius, baby; honey, I think you had enough, baby."

"Enough? When is enough, enough, angel?"

"What's wrong, Aqua-man?"

"Aqua-man, I like that. What's wrong is that I'm drunk. Well at least I think I'm drunk." "Yeah, you are drunk, waterman."

"Angel? Angel?"

"Yes, Aquarius."

"Scorpio is dead, Angel. Scorpio is dead."

"Who is Scorpio, Aquarius?"

"You mean who was Scorpio?"

"Okay, baby, okay. Who was Scorpio?"

Aquarius held up his left hand. "What's missing?"

Angel noticed his wedding band was missing. "Where is it, Aquarius? Where is your

wedding ring?"

"I gave it to a sixteen year old. I don't need it anymore."

"Wait a minute, what do you mean you don't need it anymore?"

"Just like I said, I don't need it anymore."

"Aquarius, look, it's quarter to five. You've been in here drinking since nine o'clock. And, on top of that, you haven't eaten anything all day. You have to get something in your stomach, Aquarius. Plus, you need to get some sleep."

"No, I'm alright, baby."

"Baby? You just called me baby."

"Yeah, I know what I called you; I'm not that drunk, yet."

"Am I your baby, Aquarius, or a one-night stand?"

"It's one thing about me, Angel. I do not lie. I won't lie. You know something? By me not lying, I've gotten myself into so much trouble it's not funny. I'm going to the bathroom. Which way do I go?"

Aquarius stood up, took two steps forward, then fell backwards to the floor. Angel came from behind the bar and looked down at Aquarius lying flat on his back, snoring. Angel smiled and said, "Now we are even, baby." Angel looked at Tyrone.

"Your place or the park?" Tyrone asked.

"My place, Ty, I can't have my baby in the park," she said grinning.

"I'm glad you said that, because I was going to put him in your place anyway."

"You like him too, don't you?"

"Yeah, he's got heart." Tyrone walked over to Aquarius, gently picked him up and put him over his right shoulder. Tyrone stated as he walked to the entrance of the bar, "Man is he going to have one hell of a headache when he wakes up."

"Ty, put him in my bed and come back. Okay?"

"Okay, Angel, will do."

"By the way, Ty, take his gun and lock it up for me, would you?"

"You mean guns," Tyrone replied.

"Damn! How many does he have?"

"Three. I can lock up two, the third is on you."

Angel started laughing, "Nigger, you are stupid."

"Yeah, but I'm sober, I'm gonna get me some tonight; can I say the same for you?" Tyrone burst out in a loud laugh.

"I can wait, smart ass, I can wait."

"Man, is this dude gonna catch pure hell. Better him than me."

• • • •

"How is she, doc?" Taurus asked the doctor Virgo brought to their new headquarters.

"She'll be fine. She's suffering from a mild case of stress. It's most likely from working too hard and long without a break. I gave her a mild sedative. It'll make her sleep for eight hours, at least. She needs the rest. I also gave her some pills for her to take. She's to take one in the morning and one in the evening. I gave her enough for three days. In four days, she'll be good as new."

"Thanks, doc, and thanks again for not minding the blindfold."

"Listen, if I got five thousand dollars for each patient I saw, I would come blindfolded and naked. Now, if someone will take me back to my car…"

"Oh, of course, doc." Dr. Howard Thomas was again blindfolded and Virgo led him out to the front door. Virgo opened the front door and looked left and right, and then up to make sure that the coast was clear. Once satisfied no one is watching, Virgo led the doctor to his car, opened the door and carefully sat him inside. After Virgo got settled in the driver's seat, he once again looked around and up at windows to make sure that everything was clear. Virgo never noticed the old lady looking at him from a second floor window; he started the car and pulled off.

"Damn, four days," Taurus thought out loud. "We'll just have to wait, that's all. Besides, we can all use the rest."

One hour later, Virgo returned. "What took you so long?" Leo asked.

"I drove the son-of a bitch around for half an hour then dropped him off at the hospital parking lot. Then I sat watching him to see what he was going to do."

"And?" Leo asked.

"I followed him home."

"Okay," Taurus remarked. "Okay, my ass, look out the window."

Taurus and Leo looked out the window past the white shades. "Damn!" They both watched as they saw Dr. Thomas talking to two police officers directly across the street from their house.

"Damn! The doc lives on the damn block," Taurus said in shock.

•　　•　　•　　•

It was five-forty when Rosa came into the den to announce that dinner would be served, as scheduled.

"Thank you, Rosa."

"You are welcome, Ms. Christina," Rosa said as she was leaving the den.

"Deb, want another drink?" Justina asked.

"Why, bitch? Your ass couldn't get up to get it."

"Who couldn't?" Justina asked. "I can get...I can get it. Who do you think I am, Tiny?"

Debra and Christina both looked over at their oldest sister, curled up on the sofa, knocked-out drunk. Justina was about to join her sister, when she stood up, rocking side to side. Justina took one step.

Debra screamed, "Catch her!"

"I got her," Christina said, as she caught her now youngest sister. Christina caught Justina right before she crashed face first into the coffee table. "Help me, this girl is heavy."

Debra grabbed the right side of Justina and both picked her up and gently laid her on the love seat. "I will have that drink. What about you? You want another?"

"Yeah," Christina replied, "and make Mom and Dad one; their bedroom door just opened."

Debra was just finishing up on the drinks when Tonya and Derrick entered the den. Debra handed Tonya her drink and Christina handed Derrick his.

Tonya looked Christina straight in the eyes and said, "Well?"

"I never had a doubt; I just had to break the ice between you two. Ya'll were driving us up the wall."

Tonya and Derrick both smiled.

"Yeah, well look at what a little stress can do for you," Debra remarked.

All four looked at Tynisha and Justina. Derrick slowly shook his head back and forth. Tonya squished her eyes as Justina rolled off the love seat and stretched out on the floor, getting comfortable.

"Looks like you," Tonya said, looking at Derrick smiling.

•　　•　　•　　•

The next day:

"I oughta lock up the whole bunch of you; I am very surprised at you of all people, Derrick!" Mayor Downs bellowed in his office at City Hall.

"Mr. Mayor, you of all people should know that if I knew who was behind this mess that I would have told you when it first started," Derrick said in defense of himself. "You do realize that I did lose a daughter behind this?"

"Yeah, your daughter and a dozen of cops and firefighters, not to mention the fifty-two civilians killed, including fourteen children. Plus, the sons-of-bitches blew up twelve city street corners, totaling eleven million dollars in damage and millions of dollars in lost revenue. Now you are telling me they are here to kill the top politician in the city. Derrick, the election is in three weeks...three weeks. You and your posse have twenty days. Do you hear me? Twenty days to clean this shit up. I don't give a damn how you do it, what methods you use to get it done. I just want you to get it done without making my city look like Iraq. I don't want any more dead cops, dead firefighters, or any more dead civilians. I've lost one godchild and I sure as hell don't want to lose another," the mayor said, looking at Tynisha, Christina, and Justina with a sad, pained look in his eyes. "Derrick, since you and Tonya are the only two people on earth who knows how these people think and operate, I am leaving this operation up to you. As far as any assistance from the city, you will have all the weapons needed, any needed manpower is available, and any funds are at your disposal."

"Thank you, Mr. Mayor," Derrick said.

"As far as you three," looking at Tynisha, Christina, and Debra, you are transferred."

"Transferred, sir? Transferred to what? Christina asked the mayor.

"You are transferred to Derrick and Tonya's special task force team. I talked to the State Police Commissioner and he is very upset about the whole situation, but he agreed that Justina would be safer with the task force. The commissioner felt that Justina would not be able to concentrate on her duties, knowing that a bunch of lunatics are trying to kill her family. So, as of this morning, you are temporarily transferred to my command."

Justina smiled a smile of relief.

"Tonya, As far as the FBI, they informed me that you are on assignment in California and you have your orders and they have not changed. Department commanders will be informed about the task force and will cooperate with your needs. That's all, and good luck to all of you. By the way," the mayor said with a half grin on his face, "if any of you get killed in this bullshit, you're fired. Carver, how did you get mixed up in this crap?" the mayor asked.

"It's like this, Mr. Mayor," Debra answered. "Since I was seven years old, I would come over to his house and I never wanted to leave, so he (pointing to Derrick) adopted me, and I've been getting into shit ever since."

"Get the hell out of my office!" the mayor yelled. "I have that effect on all the men I come in contact with," Debra said grinning, hurrying out of the mayor's office.

Derrick gently palmed the back of Debra's head, pulling her out the door. "Come on, child, before you get us all locked up. Let's go to the lounge and get something to eat, and I could use a drink, too. This will be your first time in the club," Derrick said, looking at Tonya.

"Actually, no," Tonya replied. "I've eaten there three times already. The food is good, a little high, but good."

"Dad, me and Deb will meet you at the lounge; we're going to check out the triplexes."

"No, J, we all go," Derrick said with excitement.

"It's alright," Tonya said, grabbing Derrick's arm. "They are long gone from there. They knew that would be the first place you would look if they were found out about."

"Look, Mom, Daddy, you two can go to the lounge and the four of us will check out the houses," Christina said.

"Two on one, make you feel better, Dad-dy?" Tynisha asked in a tiny baby tone of voice.

"Just be careful," Derrick told the women.

"Yeah, like they are going to beat all four of us. Fat chance of that," Debra said with a smirk.

"I meant to say one thing to the four of you," Tonya said in a serious tone of voice. "I ask just one thing of you."

"What's that, Mom?" Christina asked.

"When we come up against the Correctors, leave Cancer to me; she's mine. I told that bitch to leave my kids out of this shit and now my baby is gone. Her ass is mine."

"Okay by me," Justina said, "I have Ms. Libra."

"I got Aunt Teresa," Christina said.

"Good, I have Ms. Aries," Debra smiled.

"Wait a minute," Tynisha said. "Who do I have?"

"You can help me out, baby, with my bad heart and all," Derrick answered.

"That's bull, Daddy, but it's cool…it's cool," Tynisha said with a big smile on her face.

"We'll see you at the lounge," Debra said.

"Let's go," Justina said, as she got into her late-model silver BMW.

Tynisha rode with Justina.

"Race you," Christina yelled at Justina, as she got into her late-model gray Mercedes Benz.

•　　•　　•　　•

"How's Aries?" Leo asked Cancer, who has just left her room at their new location in the Society Hill section of Philadelphia. The Correctors have rented a seven-bedroom brownstone, fully furnished home, thirteen blocks southeast of City Hall.

"She's fine, still sleeping. Those pills the doctor gave her are doing their job. The only time she gets up is to go to the bathroom and to get something to eat."

"That's cool. The doc gave her six pills, how many does she has left?" Leo asked.

"Three," Cancer answered. "Tonight and tomorrow. That's fine, she will be ready to go to Water's speech rally on Saturday."

"She's fine Libra interjected. She's young and strong."

"True, true," Virgo agreed. She's not the one I'm worried about," Virgo said, turning to and looking at Teresa.

"You don't have to worry about me; I'm fine," Teresa responded quietly and politely, while staring at Cancer.

"What? Why are you staring me down? What, it's my fault Tonya screamed and passed out at her daughter's funeral?"

"She shouldn't been there at all," Teresa quietly responded.

"You forget I promised your sister, I would make sure that she saw her kids or die trying. And die is what you are going to do, too, you slimly bitch," Aries said, walking into the room in a see-thru, light blue satin nightgown, wobbly."

"You shouldn't be up just yet, Air," Leo said.

"I'm a lot better," she responded.

"Yeah, you made that promise and you took full advantage of the situation, too. You took the girl to her kid's funeral on purpose, knowing she would break down. What mother wouldn't? And then, seeing her three remaining kids all dressed in their police dress uniforms and knowing the fact that she may have to fight or maybe even have to kill one of them, bitch, please. You knew what you were doing, but let me tell you all this one thing. When they meet, and believe me they are going to meet, the rest of us stay out of it. Whoever...win, lose, or draw. That goes double for you, Teresa. I will kill the first one who interferes, so help me God, I will."

"Agreed," Teresa said, looking at Cancer.

"Agreed," the rest of the Correctors said, one after another.

"So be it, then. Cancer, when and if it comes down to just you and Tonya, you will, and you are on your own," Taurus said. "And, Cancer, no weapons."

"What? What if she has a weapon?" Cancer protested.

"She won't, trust me; she won't have a weapon, just her hands. She's going to want the pleasure of killing you with her bare hands," Teresa stated.

"Oh, so all you mother fuckers are turning your backs on me, is that it?"

"No one is turning their back on you, Cancer," Taurus defended everyone. "Remember what Tonya said? If any one of us touches any of her kids, she would kill them, including her own sister?"

"Yeah? Well, if that's the case, we are all guilty, including that slut sister of hers," Cancer snapped back.

Teresa smiled and said, "You're right, but she's only coming after you. I'm going to have to pay the price for my niece's death, but you are going to have to pay the penalty. And, the penalty for killing a cop in this city and state is death. Come on, Aries; let me help you back to bed; girl, you just made my day." Teresa grabbed Aries' waist and put her arm over her shoulder and helped her walk back to her bedroom.

With Aries and Teresa walking back to Aries' bedroom, Cancer asked, "Why just me? Why not everybody else?"

"Because you were the one and the only one mind you, threatening to kill one or more of her kids, and she did warn your black ass," answered Virgo.

"Wait a minute; wait just a damn minute," Libra said in amazement with a big grin on her face. "This bitch is scared of Tonya. She is really afraid of Tonya. All that mouth you had back at the other house was mouth, all mouth."

Teresa walked back into the room. "Hey, Gem, check this shit out. Mighty mouth over here is afraid of your little sister. I mean she is really afraid of Tonya."

"This should really be interesting," Teresa responded, "because before my sister left, she revealed to me she had doubts about beating you, Cancer. But that was before my niece was killed."

"And now?" Cancer asked. "Now I think your mouth wrote a check that your ass can't cash."

"Why, because she's your sister?"

"Yeah, but not only that; remember when Tonya came back to us?"

"Yeah and?"

"And she never took the self-defense classes with us? You thought she was afraid. Well she wasn't, she didn't need them. We were the only ones who needed them. You see, Derrick had already trained her. One day Scorpio, God bless her soul, and I sneaked into the gym and jumped her while she was practicing. Well, she beat the both of us. You remember that time when Scorp had the two broken ribs and Teresa had her right arm pulled out of the socket?"

Leo spoke up. "That was the result of a scared woman. Scorp and Teresa turned off the gym lights and jumped Tonya. When Libra and I rushed into the gym after hearing screams, we turned on the lights, finding Tonya standing over the both of them. We had to take them both to the hospital."

"But you said they were involved in a fight with some street girls," Aries said stunned, looking at Libra and Taurus.

"That was to prevent any embarrassment; who wants to admit that they were taken down by their younger sibling? And on top of that, Scorpio was the fastest and the deadliest next to Libra here," Taurus said.

"Even I didn't relish taking on someone like Scorpio. I'm bigger and stronger than any of you women, but Scorpio was lightning fast and deadly accurate. It came as a surprise when Tonya beat them both, and in the dark. Tonya never showed off skills since then," Libra finished.

"Good luck, dumb ass," Teresa said with a big grin on her face.

Cancer sat in her chair and for the first time since joining the Correctors, she had nothing to say, not one thing; everyone laughed.

•　　•　　•　　•

"How's your head?" Angel asked Aquarius, who was just waking up from yesterday's drinking binge.

"I don't know, yet...oh...there it is," he said after he tried sitting up.

"Here, drink this. It'll help your hangover."

Aquarius took the clear crystal glass filled with a bubbly clear liquid. He leaned his back against the round-shaped walnut-paneled headboard of a round-shaped king-sized bed. Aquarius noticed he was partly covered with white satin sheets. After he finished the liquid, he remarked, "It tastes good."

"I hope it's more than taste I have," Angel replied. "Or, is that more than I should hope for?"

Aquarius looks at her, puzzled. "Did I say or do something I should or shouldn't have?"

"You tell me, Aqua-man, did you?"

"First, you tell me what I did to wind up in your bed? This is your bed, right?"

"Yes, it's my bed, or our bed, depending on what you say to me."

Aquarius looked at Angel—not just looking, but staring—trying to read her face; trying hard to read her beautiful, full, round, small, chestnut complete face. Her full brown lips, medium brown eyes...no good, she was not giving him any hint, nothing. Where are my clothes and my guns? I think I better leave."

"No you don't," Angel said, as she gently pushed him back against the headboard, as he tried to get up. "It's time to stop running from your fears, your tears, your hurt, and your pain. You have a choice here, Aquarius. You cried half the night away. One, you can talk to me and I can make up my mind if I want to deal with it; or two, you can just run from your problems and chances are you'll be a drunk filled with grief and misery. Be a man and face your fears. Deal with it, Aquarius."

"If I face my... face my fears and talk to you, I just might have the chance of losing you."

"Aquarius, you don't have me, yet, anyway. Whatever you say, your chances are fifty-fifty. You can take that chance or you can walk out of my house and out of my life now."

"This may take a while, Angel."

"From the way you were talking yesterday and crying last night, I say you have nothing but time left," Angel shot back.

"What about your job at the bar?"

"I own the bar, Aqua-man. Jacks Are Wild is named after my late husband Jack. He was killed during a robbery four years ago. He was about to lock up one night, when three men came in and robbed him and the last of his customers; he went for his gun and they shot him. He left the bar to me. I have two more in the city. That's enough about me for right now. Now it's your turn and, Aquarius, don't leave anything out and don't lie to me. Don't lie."

Aquarius took a deep breath and exhaled, and started his story. After Aquarius finished, he looked and saw the soft tears running down Angel's cheeks. "Somehow, I've got to help the Centaur. I want to help him, but he may not listen. Hell, I wouldn't blame him if he didn't. But still, I have to try, even if it means him putting a bullet in my head."

"You have to try," Angel said. "Can you get in touch with that little girl again?"

"Yes, I'm meeting her tonight. We meet once a week, why?"

"Because if you want to meet and help the Centaur, and live to be with me, then I'll have to be there."

Aquarius stared at Angel in puzzlement. Then the puzzlement turned to fear.

"Aquarius, I was at Tracy Jenkins' funeral. I saw when Derrick picked that woman up and took her to the car. I am so damn glad that I didn't know your background when you came into the bar that day. You get on your knees and thank your higher power that I didn't know then, 'cause if I did, you would have not made it out alive."

Truly confused now, Aquarius began to panic. "I...I don't understand," he said to Angel.

"Tracy was my cousin, you son of a bitch. Derrick is my cousin, damn you."

"Angel!"

"Don't say a damn thing; don't say shit to me right now." The tears were now flowing harder down Angel's cheeks. Now in a full cry, Angel sitting at the foot of Aquarius on the bed, she told Aquarius, "I should blow your motherfucking brains out, but I can't. As much as I want to, I can't. Do you know why I can't?"

Aquarius sat and stared at her in pure shock.

"Answer me, goddamn you!" she screamed.

"Why, Angel? Why?"

"For two reasons. The first one is because you are not to blame, you may be a part of the people who are to blame, but you didn't kill my cousin. Two, because I care for you. For the first time in four years, I'm starting to feel alive again. The blood pumping to my heart is warm again... Warm and it's because of you. I knew you were the one when you walked into the bar that day. Then when you stood up and called Tyrone and his friends gorillas, that sealed it. Now you listen to me and you listen well. Meet that kid like you always do; but this time, you give her a message to give to Derrick.

•　　•　　•　　•

Justina and Tynisha arrived at the triplexes two minutes ahead of Christina and Debra. Justina pulled her car into the front of the houses and turned off the engine. Because it's in the early afternoon, the street is almost clear of cars usually parked there. There's only one car parked on the same side of the triplexes about seven houses down the street.

Justina and Christina started talking about the two houses. "We've haven't been here since we were kids," Justina said, looking at the house where they grew up.

Christina smiled as she looked at the ninety-year-old dwelling and reminisced about her childhood, smiling as she thought about running up and down the stairs of the three-story brick and wood building, chasing her three sisters in and out the front door; remembering when her father would hide behind the huge twin oak, glass paneled doors, painted brown and chocolate, scaring each child as they came home from school; playing house with her sisters and some girlfriends on the front lawn; and her and her sisters jumping over the two-foot high wrought iron fence that separated her house from their grandmother's next door to theirs. Christina looked up and down the quiet tree-lined street with the front lawns perfectly manicured.

Christina's train of thought was broken when she heard a car horn honking behind her. Debra was blowing her horn, as she pulled up behind Justina's car. "It's about time," Justina grinned.

"Yeah right, if you hadn't gone through that red light on Twenty-first Street, we would have beaten you here, and you a cop," Debra snorted.

"Well, come on, slowpokes; let's check out the houses and get to the lounge, I'm hungry," Justina said, grinning at the disgusted look on Debra's face.

"Deb and I will take 66 and you two check out 64," Cristina said, talking to Tynisha.

All four women drew their firearms as they cautiously approached the front door of the houses. "Let's ring the doorbells," Debra suggested.

"No!" Tynisha yelled. "Knock on the doors. I've seen too many movies where you ring the front door bell and the house blows up."

The three women looked at their big sister for a moment. "Works for me," Christina stated.

They are crazy Justina thought to herself. Justina knocked on the door. It moved to the pressure of her knock. "Hey, this door is unlocked!" Justina exclaimed.

"So is this one," Debra said.

"Should we go in?" Christina asked.

"Why not?" Debra replied.

"First, let's check for hair triggers," Tynisha said.

"Girl, you are chicken shit," Debra said.

"But not stupid," Justina added.

All four women start looking for hair triggers.

"This is stupid," Debra said, as she kicked open the door and cautiously walked into the house.

Christina told Tynisha and Justina to wait outside the house as she slowly walked into the house behind Debra. All three heard Debra cry out, "Oh, my god!"

Tynisha and Justina jumped over the railing and ran into the house. The front living room of the house was completely void of any furniture of any kind, as well as the dining area. The two women caught up with Christina in the kitchen, standing over Debra, who was bent over on one knee with her other leg stretched out on the floor. A crimson red skid mark followed her left leg.

"Tell me this is red paint and not blood," Debra pleaded in a soft, but shaky voice.

Christina, Justina, and Tynisha looked at a huge red spot and followed its trail. The trail ended at a closed door, leading to a back shed. Justina looked at Tynisha as she raised her right forefinger to her lips, as she pulled out her service weapon from its holster attached to her suit pants covered by the suit jacket. Tynisha did the same, as her sister slowly pushed open the door. "Oh shit!"

"What?" Tynisha asked.

"A dead dog, split open straight down the middle," Justina answers. "It's Mrs. Allen's Doberman; she lives next door," Justina continued.

"Didn't she have two Dobermans?" Christina asked.

"Yeah, she's had those dogs for ten years," Tynisha added.

"Damn dog's blood," Debra said sickly. There's a note attached to its dog tag.

Tynisha snatched the note and read it out loud. "Hi, sorry we missed you. But still, it's lucky for you that you picked this house to come into first. If you had come into the house next door first, you wouldn't be standing here looking at Mrs. Nosey Ass's pooch. Is it this house or is it the other house? Oh well, what the hell? I'll put it like this. We wired one of the two houses, but I forget which one. Hell, it doesn't matter. If you get out of this house alive, then we are looking forward to meeting and killing you someday. With all the hate one group of bitches can give another, Cancer."

"Okay, okay, let's figure this out," Christina told her sisters. "Is this crazy whacked out bitch screwing with our heads or is she really out of her mind?"

"Mind? Mind? Wh-what mind? Anytime a broad slits open a dog and leaves a note attached to its carcass, you know she's three cans short of a six pack. Yes, this broad is crazy," snorted Debra, wiping off her pants as much as she could with some paper towels she found in the kitchen.

"Okay then, just follow me," Tynisha said, as she turned and walked toward the front door. Tynisha stopped. "Oh no, slick ass. You won't get us this way, smart ass."

"What are you talking about?" Christina asked.

"We have to go back and out of the backdoor."

"Why, for Christ's sake?" Debra asked.

"The front door is booby-trapped," Tynisha answered.

"How do you know?" Christina asked.

"She told us."

"Who told us?" Debra screamed, annoyed?

"Shh… don't raise your voice. Ms. Cancer told us. The note she left, the word forward is underlined."

"So?" Debra asked impatiently.

"So, Deb, it's like this. We can take the chance and go out the front door or we try and go out the back. But trust me, one of them is trapped, but which one is the twenty thousand-dollar question."

"That doesn't make sense, we came into the front door and nothing happened," Justina reminded her sister.

"That's just the way they designed it," Tynisha replied. "We can come in, but we can't go out."

"Huh?" Justina asked, puzzled.

"The dog is the booby trap. You see all the rope and chains holding up the dog?"

"Yeah…and?" the other women answered at the same time.

"It doesn't take all that to hold up a hundred pound pooch. They over dressed the dog and left it as a clue to see if we were smart enough to recognize it."

"Meaning?" Justine asked.

"Meaning, little sister, we go up the stairs as they want us to," Tynisha answered.

"But if that's the case, the second floor maybe trapped as well," Christina pointed out.

"But, in this case, we have no other choice. We either go up the steps or we stay down here with our fingers stuck up our asses, looking stupid," Tynisha said.

"Lead on," Debra said to Tynisha.

Tynisha pulled her service weapon out and held it down at her right hip as she started to walk up the steps. Justina followed suit with Christina behind her and Debra behind Christina.

Tynisha noticed the blood trail going up the steps. As Tynisha reached the end of the sixteen steps, reaching the second floor, she noticed a closed door catty-cornered to her right. "Police!" Tynisha shouted. "Come out of the room with your hands locked behind your head now!" Tynisha looked down the stairs, motioning for her sisters to wait. Tynisha hand signaled for Justina to cover her as she investigated the closed room. Tynisha walked slowly to and gently pushed open the door. "It's the bedroom Christina slept in when she was a little girl. Damn."

"What?" Justina asked.

"It's the second dog. Come on up, it's clear."

The women entered the bedroom to find a second Doberman tied up like the first one on the first floor. "This one doesn't have a note on it," Debra observed.

The women were startled as the door to the front bedroom slowly opened and observed a woman standing at the entrance with a small oblong black metal canister in her right hand. "Hello ladies; my name is Cancer. Please join us."

The shocked women looked at each other.

"What is that you have in your hand, Ms. Cancer?" Tynisha asked.

"Oh, you noticed, it's just a little old trigger thing-a-ma-jig to a bomb connected to the house. Please, don't let me have to ask you again, join us."

The four women looked at each other.

"Come on, put away your pieces." The three women did as Tynisha asked.

The women slowly entered the bedroom to find two other women, sitting on fold-up chairs, each drinking a diet cola from a can. The four women noticed the room, barren of any furniture except for seven folding chairs, two of which the women were occupying, and a large round folding table. The room's walls were paneled with brown oak and the floor was carpeted with a deep plush black shag carpet.

"Please, have a seat, would you? We just stuck around since slow ass over here (pointing to her left at Gemini) actually got our asses caught. You girls grew up to be beautiful young ladies. Please forgive me, as I said my name is Cancer, to my right is Libra (Libra nodded her head) and to my left is... Hell, you already know who that is; in case you don't, this is your Aunt Teresa, aka Gemini. By the way, we do have this house booby-trapped, so just in case you ladies want to act like Bruce Lee, I suggest you get it out of your heads right now. You must understand that this remote is very sensitive."

"Close your mouth, kid, you might get a dick in it," Gemini said smiling at Christina.

"Would you ladies please put your firearms in the middle of the table? And, I do mean all of them, then have a seat and sit a week," Cancer instructed the women.

All four women did as they were told and put their service and back-up weapons on the table. The women took a chair and sat by the bay windows, Christina and Debra on the right, and Tynisha and Justina on the left.

"So, which one of you is Tynisha?" Cancer asked.

"I am Tynisha," as she stood.

"So, little niece, which one of us do you want to take on?"

"Aunt Teresa! I can't believe you can even ask me a question like that. We are family, or is that a foreign word to you? Does that mean anything at all?"

"Yeah, family means a lot to me. Why else do you think that you're still alive now? Huh, stupid ass? Answer me, stupid ass, or I'll rip your goddamn tongue out of your mouth."

"Cool down 'Gem', cool down," Libra told Gemini. "She didn't budge an inch; she's not afraid of you or us. Christina?"

"Yes," Christina answered. "I have Aunt Teresa."

Gemini smiled, "Looking forward to it, little girl. And, you are Justina."

Justina stared at Libra and said, "I'm glad I picked you, Ms. Libra, I should get a good workout with you."

"Why thank you, Justina; I look forward to kicking your ass."

Justina smiled.

Cancer then turned her attention to Debra. "And who might you be, may I ask?"

"I'm Debra. I'm adopted and I have Ms. Aries," Debra snorted.

"Oh my," Cancer smirked, as she turned to Tynisha. "You never did tell us who you have, Tynisha," Cancer said.

"Don't know, yet, I'm the cleanup woman," Tynisha grinned.

"Cute," Libra growled.

"Oh man, oh man, are we going to have a ball killing all of you," Cancer said to the women. "But the thing of it is…we can't. We would love to kill you four right now, but it can't be done."

"And why is that?" Justina asked.

"You would have to commit a criminal act against us and you've haven't, as of yet. But knowing your father like I do, it won't take too long for him to retaliate. Tell your father to back off or he will die a whole lot faster than little baby Tracy did."

"Is that supposed to be funny?" snorted Debra.

"Oh, I'm sorry, did that hurt your feelings little girl?" Cancer asked with a sarcastic tone in her voice.

"Listen, bitch!"

"Bitch? Better watch your tongue, little girl."

"Little girl? Little girl? I got your little girl. Put down your tinker toy and we'll see who the little girl is," snapped Debra.

"As much I would like to, I can't. But, I promise you one thing..."

"And? And?"

"Oh man, do I like you," Libra said to Debra. "When we meet, I promise I'll make sure that you don't die fast. I want to beat your silly young ass stupid. But right now we don't have the time to finish chatting with you. We have to leave."

"Auntie Libra?" Gemini grinned and said. "Do we have to go right now?"

"Yes, darling, but I promise you that you can kill your little playmate later. Gemini, go get the case," Libra ordered.

Gemini left the room.

"In the meantime, ladies, listen and listen well. That dead dog that you found downstairs, its blood is contaminated with poison. If any of you had any contact with its blood, you will die within twenty-four hours."

The three Jenkins women looked at Debra in horror.

"Don't panic," Libra told the women. "The antidote is in the basement, somewhere."

All the women heard Gemini cursing the attaché case for being so heavy. "Damn," Gemini said, as she entered the room. "Next time, you bring this heavy son of a bitch up with you."

"We are about to leave now, but, in order for us to do that, we have to get by you four. Open the case and let them see what's inside just for them and their neighbors."

Gemini sat the brown luggage case down flat, exposing the two leather straps it had as a safeguard in case it was accidentally opened. Gemini opened the case to reveal eight blocks of what looked like gray putty and a small round face clock (taped to one block), which was ticking.

"See, this is our guarantee that we will be able to leave without fighting you fools."

"What makes you think we won't jump anyway? You press that trigger, you will die along with us," Christina stated.

"True, true, but the fact of the matter is there is enough C-4 in that case not only to blow up both buildings, but enough to demolish the entire block, including the school down the street. Now you wouldn't want the death of all of those young school kids on your hands, now would you? Libra asked, laughing.

"You are one sick lady," Justina said to Libra. "Look Gem, your niece is not only a cop, but she's a fucking doctor, too."

"Talented, very talented," Gemini smiled. Sooo, ladies, what's it going to be? We handcuff you four clowns together so we can leave, or we can do battle and the school kids die right along with us?"

"Well, what's it going to be, ladies? Libra asked. "Oh, I'm sorry; it still doesn't look fair to you, does it? No, of course not. I'll tell you what; this is what I'll do. I will leave the cuff keys on the window sill and if you can reach them in time, you can not only save the school kids, but you can also save Ms. Debra over there. The only problem you have is we set the timer on the clock for twenty-four hours. Hey, Can? When did we set the timer? I mean how long has it been?" Libra grinned.

"Let me see," Cancer answered with a smirk. "Well, we set it at four P.M. yesterday, and what time is it now? One thirty-seven P.M.; looks like you ladies have only two hours and twenty-three minutes left and counting," Cancer laughed.

"Well, ladies, time is ticking," Libra said to the shocked and numbed women.

"Cuff us," Tynisha said, staring at Gemini.

"So glad you ladies see it our way."

Gemini and Cancer walked out of the room for a moment and returned with four sets of handcuffs. "Stand up," Cancer ordered the women. The four sisters stood and Gemini turned Debra around so her back was facing her. Debra's left hand was cuffed behind her back to Christina's right hand. Christina's left hand was cuffed to Tynisha's right hand, as her left hand was cuffed to Justina's left hand. Justina's right hand was then cuffed to Debra's right, forming a full circle. Once the women were handcuffed to each other, Libra sets one key on the sill of the left window and one on the right window sill."

"That's that," Libra said. "It's been a pleasure meeting you ladies; maybe we'll meet again. Come on," Libra ordered Cancer and Gemini, "Taurus is waiting for us. Yeah, he can be so impatient," Gemini said, laughing as she left the room. The four sisters heard the door slam as the trio exited the building.

•   •   •   •

When Derrick and Tonya arrived at the Four Sisters' Restaurant and Lounge, Derrick was shocked to learn that Angel was there waiting for him and she had a male friend with her. "I wonder who that could be," he thought out loud.

"Angel, who is Angel?" Tonya asked.

"My cousin," Derrick replied.

Patty, the head barmaid and manager, passed Derrick a handful of mail and walked away. Tonya noticed Patty, who is a very pretty blue-eyed, 5'9" tall, 150-pound Caucasian. Her medium-tanned complexion went perfect with her strawberry red hair. Patty had been working for Derrick since she turned twenty-one, and she's now thirty-five. *Damn she looks good* Tonya thought to herself. Tonya stared at Derrick.

"What?" Derrick asked.

"Are all your barmaids pretty like Patty?"

"Who, Patty? No! Patty is the ugly one."

"I heard that, boss," Patty shot back, grinning as she mixed a Tom Collins for a customer.

Derrick laughed and said, "You know you are fine."

"Well, in that case, can I have a raise?"

"Didn't I just put in an elevator just for you?" Derrick responded.

Patty just shook her head as she gave her customer his drink.

"Patty?" Patty turned around, facing Derrick. "Which bar are they in?"

"Tynisha's," she replied. "Oh boss, if that guy is here looking for a job, hire him; he's gorgeous."

"I can barely pay your salary, let alone a gigolo," Derrick responded.

"Cheapskate," Patty said smiling. Derrick and Tonya laughed.

When Derrick and Tonya entered Tynisha's bar, Tonya stopped dead in her tracks. Oh, my god!" Tonya exclaimed softly.

"What?" Derrick asked her while looking at her eyes. Derrick noticed Tonya's eyes looking straight at the young man who was with Angel.

"Hey, Cuz. What's up, Dude?" Angel asked Derrick.

"Nothing much, little girl."

"Still calling me little girl."

"That's because that's what you are, little girl." Angel smiled. "Who's your friend? Derrick asked his cousin.

"Hell, ask Tonya, it's her friend."

Derrick looked at Tonya, puzzled.

"His name is Aquarius."

"What?" Derrick asked in shock.

"Before you go off and start shooting your arrows and shit, I want you to know that I had nothing to do with your daughter's death, nothing at all; ask Tonya."

Derrick stared Aquarius in the eyes, looking for the lie; it doesn't have to be a big one, it doesn't have to be little, just a lie...period. Nothing, nothing at all, he's telling the truth.

"He's telling the truth, Derrick," Tonya said in Aquarius's defense.

"I know he is, but that doesn't excuse the fact that he's with them."

"Not anymore, sir. I was down with taking out the street drug stores and the delis, but as far as killing people just for the hell of killing them, that's not me. Never has been, never will be."

"Okay, Aquarius, tell me how or why I should believe or trust you."

"As far as why you believing me, I can't answer that; but as far as trusting me, you already know how. Only time can answer that question."

"And, in the meantime, should I have to keep watching my back?"

"That's up to you, sir; you are a former cop, you know the difference."

Derrick just stared at Aquarius. "Tell me this, Aquarius."

"Sir?"

"Why are you here and what do you want?"

"I'm here to help out, here to try to prevent the senseless death of another one of your daughters, or you, or Tonya. They will be coming after Tonya, I'm damn sure of that. As of yesterday, I'm now on their shit list. Believe me once you are targeted, you have no choice but kill or be killed."

"Now do you think I would be with someone, knowing he was responsible for my cousin's death?" Angel asked her cousin.

"I don't know, Angel, buildup does strange things to a person."

"Fuck you, Derrick!" Angel screamed. "Let's go, Aquarius, we're leaving."

"Wait. Please wait. I...I'm sorry, I didn't mean that. I didn't mean that, at all."

"Like hell you didn't; we came down here to help save your life, not to kiss your black ass, Derrick."

Derrick realized he hit a don't-go-there spot, and it would take a lot of ass-kissing to make it up to her. "Wait, really…that was uncalled for, and unnecessary. I'm very sorry, Angel. Very sorry. You have to understand that I'm under a lot of pressure. I still haven't cried for my baby girl, yet. Angel, please forgive me, please," Derrick pleaded with his favorite cousin.

"Forgive, I might, but I won't forget," Angel said, looking Derrick straight in the eyes.

"Please… Please sit down, have a seat. I'm just on edge these days."

"That's exactly why I'm here, Centaur. We hurt this city pretty bad. Those kids started this bloodshed when they killed Scorpio, Centaur, not us."

"Wait a minute, Aquarius," Derrick interjected. "That woman took out five people. Yes she did, and she died protecting a teenage girl. I've learned that sometimes the need of one outweighs the needs of many.

Derrick just sat and looked at Aquarius. Derrick looked at Angel. "Do you feel it, Cuz?"

Angel looked in Derrick's eyes and answered, "Yes. Yes, I feel it."

Derrick then turned to Aquarius and said, "Welcome to the family. It may take a little time to get used to, but what else do we have, but time? So, you are the one Angel has been running around starry eyed about?"

"I don't know about all of that, but what I do know is your cousin has a unique way with words."

"You don't know the half of it," Derrick said grinning.

"Derrick, Scorpio was Aquarius's wife," Tonya stated.

"So sorry for your loss."

"Thank you. Do you mind if we eat something while we plan how to stop the Correctors?" Angel, Tonya, and Derrick all smile.

• • • • •

"I'm going to kill that slut, as soon as I figure out how we are going to get those keys," Christina mumbled out loud.

"Okay, I have it," Justina said. "Let's all turn around with me facing the left window."

"What do you have in mind?" Christina asked.

"Since I am the tallest, I might be able to reach up to the windowsill and grab the keys."

"It might've worked, except for one thing," Tynisha said.

"What one thing?" Debra asked.

"We are all handcuffed from behind."

"So?" Christina said.

"So, we can't lift our arms up high enough for Justina to reach the damn sill. Hell, we can't even move our hands, let alone our arms."

"Shit! Shit! Shit! Shit! Why do you have to be so damn smart?" Justina asked in disgust.

"How much time do we have left?" Debra asked.

"Two hours and ten minutes left," Tynisha said, looking down at the clock attached to the explosives. ,

"Man, are we in trouble," Christina said.

"Trouble, my ass, we are dead and so are those kids at that school," Justina, interjected.

Forty-five minutes later... Hello?... Hello...is anybody there?"

"Up here," Christina and Justina shouted at the same time.

"In the second floor bedroom," Debra shouted.

The four women heard the footsteps coming up the stairs. Bonita slowly walked in through the bedroom door.

"Little girl, we are police officers; please go over to the window and get the keys to these handcuffs off the sill," Debra pleaded.

Bonita did what was asked of her. Bonita, not saying a word, picked up one of the two keys and walked over to Debra and unlocked her right wrist, and then handed her the key.

"Is that a bomb?" Bonita asked.

"Get out of here now! Wait for us outside... Go...go," Debra told the now shaking teenager. Bonita ran out of the bedroom, down the stairs, and out the front door.

After the four women were free and collected their firearms, Christina said, "Listen, Debbie and I will go down to the basement to look for the antidote, you two zip up the case and take it outside the house and wait for us."

"Like hell," Tynisha protested. "I am not touching that damn bomb; we don't know how stable that shit is."

"Look, chicken shit, if we don't get that bomb out of here kids will die; you want to live with that the rest of your life?"

"Don't be calling me names; you want to call something? Call the damn bomb squad!" Tynisha yelled at her sister.

"No time for that. Every time the bomb squad is called, it takes them an hour just to set up," Justina said, after looking down at the case. We only have forty-five minutes left."

"That's enough time for them to get here and take that thing out of here," Tynisha insisted.

"Tiny, pull yourself together, will you?" Christina asked. "Look, Tiny, you go with Debbie and look for the antidote, me and Justina will deal with the bomb, okay?"

"Okay, I can deal with that," Tynisha replied.

"Get moving, we don't have much time left," Justina stated.

Tynisha and Debra left the room and ran down the stairs to the basement.

"Damn girl, might be right about this bomb being stable," Christina said.

"Listen, don't you go and get paranoid on me, too. If Aunt Shit Head can drag this thing up the steps, we can carry it down," Justina said. Justina zippered up the case and strapped it closed. "Come on; let's get this thing to the car."

"Whoa, whose car?" Christina asked.

"You are the better driver; your car."

"I didn't drive here, remember? Debbie did."

"So, you drive Debbie's car."

"But..."

"Don't make me shoot you, girl," Justina cut her off.

Tynisha and Debra were looking around the basement to find the antidote. "Damn, this basement is clean," Tynisha observed.

"What's so strange about that?" Debra asked.

"When we were living here, we couldn't find the floor," Tynisha smirked.

"Heck, you can't find the floor in any of your rooms at your apartment now," Debra remarked.

After ten minutes of looking around the basement, Tynisha found a hidden closet with the door closed. "Deb, over here."

"What?"

"Every door in this basement is open, except this one; I wonder why?"

"Let's find out," Debra grinned.

"Wait a minute," Tynisha grabbed Debra's left hand, "you plan on opening that door?"

"Now how the hell else are we going to find out what's in there?"

"Look for hair triggers first."

"Girl, if you don't move out of the way…" Debra pushed Tynisha's hand off of hers and opened the closet door. Debra yanked the small three-foot wide door open. Both women were startled by a piece of white paper that fell to the floor. "It's a note," Debra said, as she picked it up and started reading it out loud. "'Dear stupid asses, this is to inform you that the dog's blood is not poisoned. This was planned to make you waste time. Brilliant, isn't it? Providing that the bomb doesn't go off in your faces, we will meet again. Can't wait to kill you… Er, I mean to meet you again, Cancer.' I'm going to rip that bitch's tongue and eyes right out of her face!" Debra yelled at the top of her lungs.

"Come on, let's get out of here," Tynisha said, as she turned to leave the basement. "Those women have some deep-seated issues," Tynisha said, going up the steps.

When Tynisha and Debra emerged from the house, Justina was on her car phone, talking to the police dispatcher. "Yes, we will be taking 76 all the way to the Thirtieth and Girard Avenue Bridge. We need escort once we hit 76 via Germantown Pike. You got that?"

"Yes, detective," the dispatcher answered.

"What's up? You find the antidote?" Christina asked Debra.

"There never was any antidote." Christina turns pale in the face. "No, don't worry; there was never any poison," said Debra, handing Christina the piece of paper. "They said that to make us waste time," Debra continued.

"Well it worked," Justina said, as she walked over to her sisters.

"Why do we have to go all the way to Girard Avenue?" Tynisha asked.

"That's the closes and the only area that isn't populated. Maybe by the time we get there, the bomb squad will be there to take this thing off our hands," Justina answered. "Crissy, you are driving," Tynisha informed her sister.

"Why me?" she asked.

"Because you are the only one who paid close attention during evasive driver training."

"Shit!" Christina mumbled to herself.

"This is how we are going to do this," Justina said. "Crissy, you and Debbie will follow Tiny and me. Oh yeah, this is Bonita. For now on I'm calling her St. Bonita." Bonita smiled.

"Hi, Bonita," Debra said.

"Hello, my little lifesaver," Christina said with a big grin.

"Listen, we can get formally introduced after we get rid of this bomb," Justina said with a frown. "Bonita you are riding with me and my sister Tynisha."

"Okay," Bonita agreed.

"Where's the bomb?" Debra asked.

"It's in your car," Christina answered.

"Well damn," Debra said.

"Shut up and let's get going," Justina said.

"Is she always demanding like this?" Debra asked.

"Only under pressure," Christina answered, smiling.

After All the women were sitting in their cars, Christina asks Debra, "Debra?"

"What?"

"Wouldn't it be better to hold that case in your lap so it won't bounce all over the back seat?"

"Oh shit, you're right." Debra reached over the seat, grabbed the case, and sat it on her lap.

"Open it up and check how much time we have left."

"Thirty-two minutes left."

"Thirty-two minutes left; let's roll!" Christina yelled to her sisters and Bonita.

Justina pulled off and Christina followed. "I should've taken my black ass home at night when I was little."

"Bitch, if you don't shut the fuck up…"

"Bitch? Get on the radio and let dispatch know we are rolling," Christina told Debra.

"Bitch?" Debra said out loud.

Christina gave Debra a quick hard glance.

"Okay, okay. This is Detective Debra Carver-Jenkins. We are on the move…repeat…we are on the move."

"We have been advised, detective."

"By whom, Jesus?" Debra asked in amazement.

"No, detective, by Detective Justina Jenkins."

Debra and Christina both heard Justina yell over the radio. "Debra, shut up and get off the radio."

•　　•　　•　　•

"Boss, turn on the television," Patty told Derrick when she burst into Tynisha's room.

Derrick turned on the television set: "As of right now, the two unmarked police cars are on I-76, heading south at least eighty miles an hour. Police refuse to make any comments on what's going on. There are five marked police cars escorting the two unmarked police cars, clearing a pathway to an unknown destination. We will keep you updated as this story develops."

"Oh my god, it's the kids," Derrick informed the rest of the group.

"Boss, turn on the short wave; maybe, we can get some info from the cops themselves," Patty suggested.

"Good thinking, Patty." Derrick turned the volume down on the television and turned on the shortwave radio. Derrick turned the volume up just in time so everyone could hear the message: "Mom, Dad, if you are listening, we have twenty minutes to make it to the bridge. If we make it, we'll see you at the lounge; if not, we love you two."

Derrick and company heard: "If we don't make it? If we don't make it? Bitch! If you don't get off that radio, I'll stop this car, drag you out, and kick your ass for ten minutes and still have ten minutes left to get to the bridge." The radio goes dead.

"What the hell is going on?" Derrick asked out loud.

•　　•　　•　　•

As the two cars arrived at the bridge, the bomb squad was there to take over. Debra called one of the bomb squad officers over to her. "Hey man, please take this case off my lap, and be careful, there's only eight minutes left on that clock."

"Keep still, don't move," the officer instructed Debra.

"Don't move? Don't move? Man, if you don't take this mother off my lap, I will kick your ass."

"You just keep still," the officer insisted.

"Man! Move out of the way!" Debra demanded, as she grabbed the case by its handle, gets out of the car, and walked down the empty highway, which had been cleared of any traffic to the bridge about fifty feet, and gently sat the case down in the center of the bridge. "It's all yours. I'm gonna go get drunk," Debra informed the officer, who was looking at her, shaking his head as she walked back to the car and gets in.

Christina was just finishing talking on the police radio. She started the car and made a u-turn and drove away with Justina following. "Mom, Dad, if you're listening, we're on our way to the lounge as soon as we make out our reports. See you soon, we love you and, by the way, we have your friend Bonita with us."

It was two-and-a-half hours by the time the five women arrived at the Four Sisters' Restaurant and Lounge. As they walked into the bar, the customers gave them a standing ovation, as the public had been notified that it was a bomb the women were escorting to the bridge. The five women smiled as they walked past them.

Patty informed them everyone was waiting for them in Tynisha's room. "I'll bring in drinks for you. You, you get soda," she said, smiling at Bonita. Bonita grinned back. Patty closed the door behind the women after entering the room.

"Dad, they tried to kill us," Debra broke down in tears.

"Derrick hugged Debra, "Go ahead and cry; it's your turn."

"Bonnie?" (Short for Bonita, which she preferred.)

"Mr. Aquarius?" Bonita ran over to Aquarius and he gives her a big hug. The teenager broke down into a hard cry.

Christina walked over to Tonya. Tonya held her tight.

"I'm sorry, Mom."

"Sorry? Sorry for what, baby?"

"I'm going to kill Aunt Teresa."

"Are you alright?" Angel asked Justina and Tynisha.

"No! Ms. Cancer is one dead ass," Tynisha answered as she hugged her cousin and started crying.

"I'm just fine," Justina answered, "but I'll be a whole lot better after I kill Ms. Libra."

It was the first time Derrick had ever heard his daughters speak of hurting anyone, let alone wanting to kill another human being. This time the Correctors had gone too far; the four sisters were mad.

•　　•　　•　　•

"But Leo…"

"Shut up! Shut up; don't say another word…nothing!" Leo shouted, as he slammed his clenched fist down on the six-inch thick oak coffee table and it split down the middle, the two halves falling apart on the floor. Cancer looked at the table, and swallowed, and closed her mouth.

"Just what the hell were you three thinking about when you did this?" Taurus asked.

"That's the point, they weren't thinking at all," interjected Virgo.

"They should have been!" Leo barked.

"Remember we still have to get out of the city after we do Waters, and you three fools almost blew that. I know that 'Mother' is beyond pissed off now," Aries mentioned.

"Hell, I would be," Taurus said.

"We just thought that maybe by taking out his three other brats at one time would take all the fight outta him," Libra protested.

"When did you become so cold?" Virgo asked.

"She's been around Cancer too damn long and it's beginning to rub off on her," Taurus stated. "Listen, no more pranks, no more setups, no more anything until we do Waters. Do you three understand?" Taurus asked Cancer, Gemini, and Libra.

"Understood 'T'," Libra answered.

"Understood," Gemini said.

"Whatever," Cancer said, walking out of the room.

"Something is definitely wrong with that woman," Taurus said.

•　　•　　•　　•

The next day:
Derrick and company spent the night at the Four Sisters' Lounge. Derrick felt his girls had just gone through too much stress and trauma for them to be alone at their own homes. At five A.M., Derrick and Aquarius were having coffee and talking.

"Mr. Jenkins, I..."

"Call me Derrick," Derrick cut Aquarius off.

"Okay, and me, Tony. Derrick, I can't see Taurus ordering a hit on all three of your girls like that. Knowing you lost one child already; I can't see that at all. He knows that would only make matters worse for him and the team. Besides that, he's the godfather of all of your girls; he loves the hell out of those women. You should have seen the look on his face when he found out that your baby girl was killed; we thought he was going to have a heart attack. We all heard him crying in his room that night, he was hurt. I bet he didn't have anything to do with it."

"You know something, Tony? I'm betting that they planned that mess behind his back. Leo is cold, but not that damn cold. Cancer, I'm a betting man... I bet Cancer planned the hit."

"Okay, I'll go along with that, but that doesn't explain why Libra was there or Teresa. Teresa's their aunt, for goodness sake. Libra must have been caught up in the web somehow, 'cause normally she won't fight you unless it's one-on-one, let alone kill someone who can't defend him or herself. Teresa, I don't know about her. Over the years, she's become colder and colder. More distant, more to herself here lately; I just don't know, Derrick, I just don't know."

Both men hear footsteps on the stairwell, and look up to see Justina coming down the stairs. She joined both men. "Good morning, Daddy, Aquarius."

"Good morning, baby," Derrick replied.

"Good morning, Justina."

"You studied our files hard, didn't you, Aquarius?"

"Was my job."

"What's your job now?"

"The same as yours."

"Is it?"

"I'll die before I let them kill another member of your family, if I can help it."

Justina sat across the table from her father and right next to Aquarius. Can I have some coffee, please?"

"Sure thing, Justina," Aquarius answered, as he poured her a cup of black coffee. "Cream and sugar?" Aquarius asked.

"No thanks. I like my coffee black like me, and I'm already sweet, until I get mad," she said, looking Aquarius straight in his eyes. "You know something, Aquarius? I wanted to kill you last night. I wanted to blow you away as soon as my mom introduced you to us. I wanted to kill you, even after Mom told us you are here to help us stop the Correctors. I wanted to kill you, even after you said if it meant your own life. When I went to bed, I started crying, crying because I couldn't kill you; crying because of my baby sister Tracy; crying because Aunt Teresa is a part of the Correctors; and crying because I know we might have to one day kill her. I was crying when Angel came into my room, and you know something? She didn't try to stop me from crying; she said, 'You go, girl. Go ahead and cry your heart out. Get it all out, Cuz. You do know that you're not the only one. I wanted to blow that fine son of a bitch's head off, too.' Then she told me what you told her." Justina stopped and took a sip of her coffee.

"And now, Justina?" Aquarius asked.

Justina stood up from the table and looked down at Aquarius. She looked at him for almost two minutes. Aquarius said nothing, but looked Justina in the eyes.

"Stand up, Aquarius."

Aquarius stood up facing Justina. Justina hugged Aquarius and gave him a kiss on the cheek. "Welcome to the family."

"Thank-you, Justina," Aquarius sighed with relief.

Angel and Tonya were at the top of the stairs, looking over the banister at what was going on between Aquarius and Justina. "Yes, yes, yes..." Angel said out loud.

Derrick looked up and smiled. "That's only one; you still have three more to go," Tonya reminded her.

"Yeah, but cousin, I got the hardest one first."

Tonya and Angel joined the trio at the table. After Tonya and Angel sat down, they both gave Aquarius a wink and a smile. Aquarius returned the winks and the smile. Derrick laughed. After exchanging good morning greetings, the subject changed to Bonita and Debra.

"That little girl saved our lives yesterday," Justina began. "Angel, she is crazy about your man. Girl, you have a problem on your hands."

Aquarius blushed.

"I can handle it," Angel said grinning.

"You did let her parents know that she's here and all right?" Tonya asked Derrick.

"I did that last night," Derrick spoke up. "Her parents will be here at two to pick her up. I've arranged for Bonnie and her family to go on a two-week cruise before school reopens."

"Derrick, that was really a nice thing to do," Tonya said.

"It was the only thing I could really think of to keep the child safe."

"Well, Cuz, you did the right thing," Angel said.

"You're saying that because you don't want to lose your man to a sixteen-year-old," Justina said laughing.

"Damn right," Angel replied.

"Good morning, everybody."

"Good morning," everyone responded.

It was Christina coming down the steps, followed by Debra and Tynisha, who is yawning. The three women took a seat at the large, long park picnic-style table. Debra started counting to eight. "Where's the lifesaver?"

"Still sleeping," Christina responded. "She had quite a night."

"Thank God for your little girlfriend, Aquarius," Tynisha said grinning. "Excuse me, Angel, but two's company three's a crowd."

"Go to hell, Cuz," Angel replied.

"Quote: been there, done that; didn't like it, not going back, unquote," Tynisha said. Everyone laughed.

"I smell food, I'm starving," Christina said.

"Rosa and Tommy (the head cook) are here with two more cooks. They're making breakfast. Rosa is mad. She is not happy with last night," Derrick told the group.

"She's not happy," Tynisha said smiling.

"Daddy…," Tynisha started off. "Those women are crazy. I don't mean throwed off, I mean downright, 100 percent loony tune. That makes them very dangerous. I was hoping that we could capture and bring them in alive. No such luck," Tynisha continued. "The only way they are coming in is in body bags, including Aunt Teresa, Mom."

"I agree," Derrick spoke up. "Last night showed me that they don't care who they hurt and that they won't allow anyone to get in their way, including family…Tonya."

"Well, Derrick, we've all have chosen the side we want to be on; they have got to be stopped…stopped at any cost."

"You do realize that we do have a choice here," Tonya pointed out.

"And what's that, Mom?" Justina asked.

"We could let the Correctors do Waters and save the rest of the city from any further bloodshed. Of course, that means letting Tracy's death be in vain. Or, we can put our lives on the line and stop them somehow."

"Hell, Mom, that's not a choice," Debra spoke up.

"We are dammed if we do, and dammed if we don't. Besides, I for one want my crack at Ms. Aries. I want Aunt Teresa even more now than I did before," Christina said.

"I'm going to stop Ms. Libra dead in her tracks, and I do mean that literally," Justina said with a frown on her face.

"I'm sorry, Mom, but after what Ms. Cancer did to us, she's mine, for my baby sister and me. I'm going to knock that silly grin of hers upside down," Tynisha said to Tonya.

"Okay, baby, you can have Cancer," Tonya agreed.

"Thanks," Tynisha smiled. "Daddy?"

"Yes, Tynisha."

"Daddy?"

"Yes, Christina."

"Daddy?"

"Yes, Debbie."

"Daddy?"

"Yes, Justina."

"As far as you are concerned, when we meet these women, we are no longer your little girls. We are police officers. You've got to think of us as police officers, or you will get us all killed. Do you understand, Daddy? I'm telling you this for one reason. You are not going to like hearing or seeing what your children will become. Agreed, Daddy?" Christina asked her father.

"Agreed," Derrick answered.

"As for you, Debbie," Derrick began, "we are naming the front bar, Debbie's Hideaway."

Debra smiled. "Hot damn, I have a hideaway in my name."

"No, fool! You now own Debbie's Hideaway," Christina stated.

Debra sat stunned and shocked, as tears started rolling down her cheeks.

"Now that's only the second time since second grade that I've seen you cry," Christina quoted.

"Well, don't get used to it. It will be the last time too…in your lifetime anyway," Debra grunted.

"Wanna bet?" Christina asked.

"Fifty dollars," Debra grinned.

"Bet," Christina responded, as the two shook hands and everyone laughed.

It was eight-thirty when Bonita came down the steps, rubbing her eyes. "Good morning," she said.

Everyone stood up and began clapping. Bonita smiled as she entered the room. Bonita looked over at the table and spotted Aquarius; she noticed an empty spot next to him. The teenager walked around the table past Angel to the spot and sat down next to Aquarius. Bonita said with a smile, "Good morning, Mr. Aquarius."

"Good morning, Bonnie," Aquarius answered with a smile. Angel shook her head smiling, as everyone laughed.

It was seven-thirty by the time everyone was just about back to his or her regular selves. Bonita's parents picked up their daughter at two o'clock so they could start preparing for their cruise the following week. Aquarius gave Mr. and Mrs. Harrison a ten thousand dollar check for spending money. Bonita gave Aquarius a hug and a kiss on the cheek.

Derrick and his family decided to stay at the lounge for the time being, each for their own reasons, which they kept to themselves. Derrick pleaded with Angel to stay at the lounge with Aquarius. Angel agreed, but she had to go and check in at Jacks Are Wild, so her friend and bodyguard Tyrone wouldn't be looking for her. Derrick asked everyone to be back at the lounge by midnight, but cautioned them to be careful, and to travel in pairs or more for their own safety. At midnight everyone was back at the lounge.

It was eight-thirty when Rosa was finished clearing the dinner dishes and making sure that everyone was comfortable. Derrick told Rosa everything was fine and to go home, but Rosa refused. Rosa told Derrick, "Those are my girls, too; if you want me to go home, fire me."

Derrick gave Rosa a kiss on the cheek and said, "I give up." He knew it would be pointless to argue with Rosa; once she got mad, she stayed mad for a period of time, depending on the situation. It would be a while before she calmed down.

Derrick told everyone about the time a burglar broke into the house and was stealing silverware and other things in the house in Roxborough. After the thief packed what he could, he went into the kitchen and fixed himself a sandwich and got a beer. This fool had nothing else better to do than to eat and go lay down to sleep. Rosa, who had heard the noise from her bedroom, found the fool in the living room on the couch snoring. She woke the fool up and then commenced beating his ass. Mind you, she never did call 9-1-1. She made this idiot put all the stuff he had bagged back into its place and told him he was going to pay for the sandwich and beer he ate and drank. He told her that he didn't have a job and he couldn't find one. Rosa told him she would help him find a job and he would pay her for the sandwich and beer.

"Well, Daddy, did he get a job and pay up?" Christina asked.

"Ask him for yourself."

"Huh?"

"Rosa, would you tell the head cook to come here for me please?"

The four women were in shock when Tommy came into the room. "But, Daddy, that's Rosa's husband," Justina said smiling.

"Yes, it is. When I come home from work every day since I hired Rosa, she would make me eat breakfast. So, when this man came into the kitchenette and served me my food, I just figured it was just a new guy Rosa hired. I told Rosa to hire a dishwasher; although we had an automatic one, Rosa would never use it, she didn't like it. When I tasted the food, I asked Rosa what did she do, change her recipe? That's when she told me about the incident that happened that early morning. I got mad; I wanted to lock his ass up. But, Rosa, with all her wisdom, convinced me to give him a chance. They were married five years later.

"Rosa, you sly old fox," Tynisha said with a gleeful twinkle in her eyes.

Rosa blushed and left the room. Since Rosa wouldn't leave, neither would Tommy. Rosa sent the other two cooks home and told them to be back at six-thirty the following morning. Since the lounge had twelve rooms with two beds in each and their own private bathrooms, there was enough room for everyone. Patty had the booking officer for the lounges refuse any bookings due to family tragedy until further notice. With all eight sitting at a long table, sipping various drinks in front of them, Derrick told everyone, "Listen up everyone. I've figured out a way that maybe we can put an end to this madness."

"How's that, Derrick?" Tonya asked.

"I've invited the Mayor and his chief of staff to come here tonight at ten o: clock, I'll tell you then, so I don't have to repeat myself. So, don't get happy with the joy juice. I want everyone to be alert for what I have to say. I just hope it works," Derrick mumbled to himself.

•　　•　　•　　•

At the same time:
"Are you sure it was him, Libra?" Leo asked.

"Yeah, it was him, Leo."

"I was with her," Aries answered. "It was Aquarius with Tynisha and another woman he was holding hands with."

"So, fish brains has a new mermaid; I guess we are going to have to kill her right along with him," Cancer said with smirk. Everyone looked at Cancer and shook their heads in disgust.

"Don't you ever get tired of killing?" Gemini asked.

"I'll let you know after I do your yellow ass," Cancer answered sarcastically. Gemini replied smiling, "You wish."

"Did you see where they were going or coming from?" Taurus asked.

"No, traffic was too heavy to make a u-turn to follow them; they were walking across the street," Libra answered.

"Where was this?" Virgo asked.

"About three miles north of City Hall," Aries answered.

"It looks like a rooster has flown the coop," Virgo said with a serious, disgusted frown on his face.

"Man, he knows every spot on our hit trail," Aries complained.

"I, for one, say we should leave him alone; he's suffered enough with the loss of Scorpio," Gemini commented.

"What? What the hell are you talking about?" Cancer asked in shock. "We've lost three members already. Isn't that enough? We have never lost any members; it's an omen, leave well enough alone," Gemini said. "As long as he doesn't get in the way of our job, we leave him alone. If he interferes, then we kill him and not before," Gemini continued.

Taurus looked at Gemini dumbstruck, but giving some thought to what she said.

"I second that motion," Libra said.

"I third it," Aries spoke up.

"Done, Aquarius is not to be touched unless we positively have no choice," Taurus said.

"It doesn't matter if Aquarius knows the hit trails, they won't be able to cover all of them anyway," Leo spoke up.

"No? What about the cops?" Cancer asked.

"There won't be any more cops than normal," Taurus added.

"How do you figure that?" Virgo asked.

"Because, thanks to that little stunt the three stooges pulled, the Centaur has by now taken this thing personally," Taurus said.

"Hell, he probably started taking it personal after his child got killed, I would have," Virgo commented.

"He couldn't, no matter how he felt on the inside," interjected Leo.

"I don't understand," Cancer admitted. "Why couldn't he?" she asked.

"She was a cop, and she was on duty. She was working when she got killed," Leo told Cancer and all listening. "But, when you three clowns made that move on his other girls, that's when he took it as a personal attack against him," Taurus added.

"They were armed, Taurus," Cancer snapped.

"Of course, they were armed. All Philly cops are armed; on or off, they have to be. Let me explain," Taurus said. "All cops are usually armed on or off duty, because they never know when they may meet up with some deranged nut, who just got out of the pen and wants revenge."

"Well, that's all the better for us," Libra said.

"No, not really. It leaves us vulnerable and uncovered. If I know the Centaur, and I do, he's going to let his girls do their jobs or the girls themselves will insist on it."

"Meaning?" Teresa asked.

"Meaning, the Centaur's three girls and that other woman will be covering four spots, Tonya and the Centaur will be covering two more. That leaves just one spot open," Virgo said.

"Yes and that one spot will be covered by Aquarius, if he is working with them," Leo commented.

"That means no one will be able to have anyone's back," Aries acknowledged.

"We will be on our own at Waters' rally this Saturday," Cancer protested.

"We all know what we have to do, if Aquarius isn't there, fine; if he is, kill him, but everyone be careful," Taurus pleaded.

"Aries, you know what you have to do," Leo spoke directly to her with a snide grin on his face.

"Yes, I do," Aries said grinning.

Taurus looked puzzled, but didn't say anything. Perhaps Leo would tell him when the time comes. He'd done this type of thing before; he just shrugged it off.

$$\bullet \quad \bullet \quad \bullet \quad \bullet$$

The mayor, along with his chief of staff, arrived at the Four Sisters' Lounge at ten o'clock. After all the greetings and introductions were over, the ten of them sat down to do business. "Mr. Mayor, I believe I've found a way to end this insanity, but I need your help in doing it."

"Whatever I can do, Derrick, what's on your mind?" Mayor Downs asked.

"I want to put an ad in the morning papers, all the papers."

"What kind of ad?" the Mayor asked.

"Excuse me for a minute, sir," Timothy Roberts interrupted. "You called us all the way here to ask if you can run an ad in the morning newspapers, Jenkins?"

"No, let me explain," Derrick cut off the short, 5'5", round, pudgy, light-skinned black man of around forty-five years old.

Roberts had been the mayor's chief of staff since the mayor was elected. The mayor himself disliked the man personally, but he knew what he was doing. He so much knew what he's doing that Waters had already asked him to stay on when he got re-elected. Roberts was married with four children, two girls and two boys. The girls were the oldest, twenty-three and nineteen, and the two boys were fifteen and eleven. It's the way we communicate. You see, I put an ad in the four major newspapers asking for a meeting; if they agree, they will post an ad in the papers the next day."

"What does this ad consist of, Derrick?" Roberts asked. "Greetings?"

An irritated Derrick answered. "What we do is we take out a full-page ad, consisting of my Zodiac sign, with an insertion of where we will meet. If they agree, they will answer with an ad and the Zodiac sign of the person with whom I, or we, will have the meeting."

"Where we need your help is we need your influence to make the ad priority one. Besides that, we have to do this alone. We cannot have any police involvement at all. Some of those people hate cops more than the others."

"Why tomorrow, Derrick?" the mayor asked.

"I want to divert some attention away from Waters on Saturday, Your Honor," Derrick answered.

"Do you think they will try and kill Waters on Saturday?" Downs asked.

"No, Your Honor, they won't," Tonya answered, seeing that Derrick was getting impatient with Roberts.

"The contract is for Election Day and on Election Day only," Tonya answered with a tone of resentment for Roberts in her voice. "If Waters is killed before Election Day, it's from another faction."

"How can you be so sure that they won't strike early?" Roberts asked.

"Because Waters is still alive today. Besides, they won't breech the contract, Mr. Mayor, never have, and never will," Tonya responded.

"You do realize if Waters dies between now and Election Day, so does this city," the mayor pointed out to both Derrick and Tonya.

"Your Honor?"

"Yes, Christina?"

"You don't have to worry about Mr. Waters Saturday. My sisters and I will be right there to watch over him. Trust us, God Dad," Tynisha said smiling.

Yo, GD (God Dad), we got this," Justina said grinning.

After thinking for about two minutes, the mayor looked at Roberts. "What do you think?"

"I don't like it," Roberts answered.

"Shit, man, you don't like yourself. So, I know damn well you don't like my dad's plan," Debra snapped at Roberts. "Hell, you're one of those kind of niggers; if you didn't think of it, it's no good. Dad, Your Honor, the plan is sound and it's safe; go with it, it's the way to go. Fuck that fat bastard; he didn't lose a sister or a daughter to these maniacs!" Debra screamed while crying. "I warn you, Roberts, if anyone in this room gets killed because of you, I will kill you myself, do you hear me? I swear to God, I will kill you."

"Take her upstairs!" Derrick shouted to no one in particular.

"I've got her," Tonya said, as she grabbed Debra, who was now crying uncontrollably and led her toward the stairs. Tonya turned to the mayor and Roberts, "Forgive her; she's been under a lot of stress."

Roberts, who was visibly shaken, sat on the chair in a state of shock, and said nothing else.

"Mr. Mayor…," Derrick began.

"Derrick, run your ad," the mayor cut him off. "There will be normal police coverage on Waters Saturday, but I pray for both our sakes that this thing works."

"Mr. Mayor, if they wanted to breech the contract, Waters would have been dead by now; trust me, I know these people," Derrick pled his case.

"Derrick, is there somewhere we can have a few moments alone?" the mayor asked.

"Sure, Your Honor, come this way," Derrick replied, as he led him out of Christina's room into Debbie's Hideaway where Patty worked. "Mr. Mayor, have a seat," Derrick told him, pointing to a booth. "Would you like a drink?"

"After that exchange, yes I would; bourbon on the rocks, make it a double, would you please?" Patty nodded her head.

Derrick sat down across from the mayor and started to try and explain Debra's actions.

"No, Derrick, the fat fuck had that coming to him. Personally, I can't stand the fat fuck myself."

Patty came to the booth with the mayor's drink and a double on the rocks for Derrick.

Thank you," the mayor said to Patty, as she started to walk away.

"You are very welcome," Patty said to the mayor.

The mayor gave Patty a twenty-dollar bill.

"Oh, no sir, the drinks are on the house," Derrick said.

"It's not to pay for the drinks, Derrick."

Patty looked at her boss. Derrick nodded his head in agreement."

"Thank you, Mr. Mayor."

"Oh, you know who I am?"

"Yes, sir, I voted for your opponent."

"Smart girl," the mayor said, as Patty walked away.

"Derrick, did you feel the anger in that child's voice? Did you really hear the hurt and pain, plus the frustration? Did you hear it, Derrick? I am so glad that I won't be on the other side of that fence, when Carver and my god kids climb over it to get to those people. It won't be a pretty sight. I asked for us to be alone for one reason. Tell Carver and my god kids that when they complete their mission, that they will be sergeants when they come back from their month-long vacations. I love what Carver did, I just love it. Tell Carver to watch her back when it comes down to Roberts. After what she did, I would keep my eyes open when it comes down to him, he can be pretty nasty and mean. And, the little bastard is sneaky on top of it, too." The mayor swallowed his drink and stood up. "Tell the fat fucker to come on, we are leaving, before I sit up in this bar and get drunk and really tell the son of a bitch what I really think of him. No, let me go back in there and say so long to my god kids and everyone else."

After the mayor and Roberts left, Derrick looked at his girls and the rest of the group. "Don't worry about it, Daddy, we'll work it out; we'll work it out," Tynisha assured her father.

Derrick then looked up to the stairs.

"Don't go up there, Daddy, Mom has that," Christina said.

"Come on then, let me buy everybody a drink."

"Deb? Talk to me, baby. Talk to me so you can feel better," Tonya pleaded.

"Mom, I know Daddy hates me right about now."

"No he doesn't, how can you think such a thing, little girl?"

"I almost blew Dad's thing tonight."

"No you didn't, Deb. You were probably the only one of us who saw something tonight. It's called insight, baby. We all have it, but we only see things when they need to be seen. You were the only one to see right through Roberts tonight. You ripped through him like a hot knife going through butter. I just want you to let whatever you are holding onto on the inside, I want you to let it out, honey. Deb, if you don't let it out, it will hurt you and hurt you until it can't hurt you any longer. But the thing of it is, when you no longer feel the pain, when you are numb to any sensations of any kind, such as hope, happiness, or love, then, baby, you know then that you have died. Yes, died. Don't let that happen to you. You are too young to die, little girl, you are still a baby. You might wonder how I know. Well, let me tell you how I know. I was dying myself. I almost killed my own husband."

Debra sat up on the bed and looked at Tonya strangely. "What the heck are you talking about, Mom?" Debra asked Tonya.

"Yes, Deb, I almost killed your father." Tonya then told Debra how Derrick and the kids came to Philadelphia. When Tonya finished her story, Debra was just staring at her new mother. "But, I was lucky. I was brought back from the dead. Your father showed me that it is alright to make mistakes. Derrick showed me that I am, after all I've done in life, I am nothing but a human being. To be human is to be happy, to be sad, to be loved and to love, to hate and to be hated, and to have pain and to be painless. It's okay to smile one minute and to frown the next. It's okay to live, but you must remember one thing. When you were born and inhaled your first breath of air, you signed a contract with your higher power. That contract is in order to live you must die. However, what you do between living and dying is up to you. Just like that first breath of air, trust me, you will take the last. What I am trying to tell you is that you don't have to live life in pain.

"But, it's up to you, my outspoken little girl," Tonya said, as she stood up and started walking to the bedroom door.

"Mom, wait." Tonya turned and looked at Debra. "Mom, can I tell you something?"

"Child, you can tell your mom anything. Remember this one thing, then I'll shut up and listen to you. Good parents will tell their child or children this one thing. No matter how big or how small, you can come and discuss anything with me or us."

"Mom, did Dad tell you how he came to adopt me?"

"No, and I didn't ask either, why?"

"You don't care or mind that Dad took on the responsibility of taking on another mouth to feed? Or to raise another child, and a girl at that?"

"Damn, child, you don't eat that damn much, do you?" Debra broke out in a big smile. "And, as far another girl, he will tell you himself, he would rather have another girl than to have a boy."

"And, why is that?"

"It should be obvious; if you were a boy, then he would have to worry about your hormones running wild during puberty. So, talk to me, child of mine."

"From the first time I met Christina when we were in the second grade, we hit it off real good. I had a black eye, and Crissy had a bleeding nose and busted lip."

"When you said you hit it off well from the start, you really meant that literally, didn't you?" Tonya asked.

"Yes, I did," Debra answered with a grin. "From that day on, we were like two peas in a pod. Every time Dad saw me, I was over his house. I was either driving Rosa up the wall, or I was getting on Daddy's nerves… his last nerve, mind you. Sometimes Dad would throw me out and Crissy would sneak me back in through her bedroom window."

"Debra, Christina's room is on the second floor."

"I know that, Mom, why do you think that stupid tree isn't in the back yard anymore?"

"What happened to that tree, anyway?"

"Daddy had it chopped down after I fell out of it and broke both my arms and my right leg."

"You did what?" Tonya said in shock.

"That's not all, Mom; Crissy got jealous of all the attention I was getting, so she climbed up the tree and jumped out of it. She just broke one arm. Daddy was furious; he not only had the tree chopped down, he put me and Crissy on punishment for two months and my mom and dad went along with it. Mom, those hospital bills were in the thousands. One night, I heard my mom and dad talking about money; that night felt strange to me for some reason I didn't understand. I knew something was wrong when both my mom and dad came into my room to tuck me in. They always did it one-by-one. Around four o'-clock in the morning, I heard the gunshots. I was so scared, I couldn't scream. The last thing I remembered was Daddy picking me up from off my mom and dad's bedroom floor. I was told my mom and dad shot themselves to death, after they went bankrupt. Mom, we didn't need the money, as long as we were together, and had each other, everything would have been fine. That happened when I was seven. The next thing I knew, I had four brand new sisters. Mom, I was an only child. What I didn't know was two weeks earlier, my mom and dad had asked Daddy if anything had happened to them, would he adopt me? Daddy told them I was already adopted, and they were only borrowing me so they wouldn't be lonely."

"What kind of work did your parents do, Deb?"

"They were bankers." Tonya sat stunned. "Messed up, isn't it?" Tonya said nothing.

"Debra, what was that about downstairs with Roberts?"

"Mom, that son of a bitch was at the scene the night of my parents' death. Tonya could see the hatred for Roberts in Debra's eyes. He was a cop back then. He was laughing and joking. I overheard him tell one of the detectives, two bankers who couldn't manage their own money; I'm glad I don't bank at the banks they worked at. Hell, I might have gone bankrupt. When he got promoted to captain, he had five good cops fired because they wouldn't do things his way. I'm talking about veteran cops with twenty or more years. They almost lost their pensions. If it wasn't for the appeals board, they would've. His motto is 'My way or the highway'."

"But that still doesn't explain why you almost took his head off."

"Five years ago when Crissy and I joined the force, he tried to keep me from getting on. Why? He told the director of personnel that my parents were off, in a manner of speaking. He said that apples don't fall far from the tree. Daddy got mad and by being an inspector, he had me go to a special mental clinic for city personnel."

"What happened then?"

"I passed with flying colors. The doctor said that I was fit and sane. But after a few years on the force, it might be a different story. Roberts was mad that Daddy intervened; he's been after me every since. If it wasn't for Daddy, I might've been fired a long time ago. Lucky for me, Roberts went to work for the mayor at the same time Daddy retired from the force. Mom, I love my dad and my sisters. I already lost one sister and am not about to lose another..."

"Debra, don't even think like that. If it's God's will, all will be fine. Lie down and go to sleep, you will feel much better tomorrow."

"Yeah, if Daddy don't kill me in my sleep first."

"Debra!"

"Yes, Mom?"

"Shut up and go to sleep, before I kill you myself," Tonya said grinning.

"Mom?"

"Yes?"

"I love you, too," Debra said with a grin. "I love you too, little girl, now go to sleep."

"Good night, Mom."

"Good night, Debra," Tonya said, as she turned off the light and closes the door.

• • • •

"Smooth, Centaur, real smooth," Leo laughed. "I like your style, you're slick as oil. You've got to hand it to him," Leo said, as he handed the early morning edition of one of the local newspapers to Taurus, "he's not stupid."

"No! He's never been that," Taurus replied as he read the ad in the middle of the newspaper. "He made sure that we see that ad two days before Waters rally on Saturday."

"What does that ad mean?" Aries asked.

"It means the Centaur is afraid that we might go after Waters Saturday. Sending that ad, asking for a meeting, is his way of trying to sidetrack us," Teresa responded.

"Yeah, but surely Tonya has already told the Centaur that the contract is to be fulfilled on Election Day," Libra stated.

"He wants to size us up," Cancer implied. "He wants to know what frame of mind we are in. Are we cool, calm, and collected, or are we two cans short of a six-pack."

"Well put," Taurus agreed with Cancer.

"If that's the case, he already knows that three of us are brain dead. He wants to see how the rest of us are holding up," Virgo added.

"You want to go, Leo?" Taurus asked.

"No, you go. You know he and I don't hit it off. One of us might wind up dead, or maybe the both of us."

"I vote that we don't go," Teresa said. "It might be a trap, a setup, that whole area might be flooded with cops."

"I don't think so," interjected Taurus. "If it's one thing the Centaur has, it's honor. He doesn't believe in treachery."

"Well, what are we going to do?" Leo asked.

"Aries, you go to the rally on Saturday as planned. Virgo, you and Leo go with her as backup. Cancer, you stay here just in case the Centaur has changed. Cancer, if none of us are back by midnight, kill Waters at your own leisure. I'll meet the Centaur. Libra and Gemini will be my backup."

"You realize my nieces might be there, right?" Teresa asked.

"Yes, I realize that, but they will be there as backup for their father," Taurus answered. "Then again, they just might be there for Waters, protecting him; who knows? I just want to know what the Centaur has on his mind. Alright, everybody, keep alert, no sneak attacks, no surprises, no nothing. There will be too many cops at the event to get gun happy or otherwise," Taurus ordered. "The Centaur wants to meet at Love Park. Virgo?"

"Yeah?"

"Find out on the city street map where Love Park is located."

"Will do," Virgo answered.

"Okay, Centaur, you want Love Park, Love Park it is. Do your thing 'A'."

"Gotcha 'T'," Aries said, smiling as she reached for the phone to answer Derrick's ad.

"Listen, people, we have only seventeen days left until Election Day. Don't screw this up."

•   •   •   •

"I'm sorry, Derrick, but I don't like it. I have an eerie feeling about this whole meeting setup."

"Listen, from what my cousins just went through the other day, do you think you can trust them?" Angel questioned her cousin.

"I have no choice in the matter, the cards are dealt and I have to play them or fold. Besides, Taurus is in control and I do trust him."

"Okay, that's fine and well you trust him, but what the hell makes you think he's in charge?"

"I think that because the city is still intact and not burning down around us, Angel!" Derrick answered testily.

"Don't be getting attitude with me because I'm concerned about you and my cousins."

Derrick stared at his cousin. "Okay, Angel, what's up? Why are you so afraid?"

"Oh, what are you saying, Derrick? Are you saying that I can't feel for my family's safety?"

"Don't bullshit me, Angel, you're worried about Aquarius. Don't tell me you're not, either, your legs have been knocking all morning. You've been nervous since you got up, walking up and down the stairs. Hell, you've been pacing back and forth. You're doing and acting the same way you did when Jack..."

"Go to hell, Derrick," Angel shouted as she turned and ran up the stairs to where the bedrooms were, brushing past Aquarius, crying.

"What's going on," Aquarius asked no one in particular.

"On the day Jack was killed, Angel woke up that morning sweating like a pig. She was soaked to the bone. She was shaking like a leaf on a windy day. Her nerves were shot. Like my dad said, she was all messed up the entire day. She kept repeating, begging Jack not to go to work that night. She told him if he went to work that night that it would be the last time she would see him alive. He laughed and assured her he would be alright. He told her, besides, he couldn't or wouldn't let one of his employees take a fall if it was meant for him. That night, Jack was gunned down," Christina answered tearfully.

Derrick felt one-inch tall.

"There's one more thing," Justina added. "Before Jack went to work that night, Angel made him make love to her. She wanted to get pregnant so she would have something, or I should say a son or a daughter to remind her of him; someone that truly was her own and no one else's."

"And did she, get pregnant I mean?" Aquarius asked.

"Yes, she did," Tynisha answered.

"What happened? Where is the child?" Aquarius asked.

"She lost the babies, twins. She couldn't hold them; it was her nerves," Derrick softly answered. "Go to her, Aquarius, go to her. Do one better than that," Derrick added. "Stay here with her; she needs you now more than we do at the rally. Tony, don't go out here today. You and Angel both stay inside. If you two need anything, Rosa or Patty will help you with it. Besides, if they were to spot you at the rally, they just might shoot you, cops or no cops."

Aquarius looked at everyone, one after the other, looking for approval. Each one nodded their head approving Derrick's decision. Aquarius, without saying a word, stood up and walked to the stairs without looking back; he didn't want them to see the teardrops running down his face.

Derrick looked at his watch. "Twelve o'clock, let's go everybody, we have work to do. Wait a minute, let's just go over this one more time," Derrick said. "I'll meet Taurus; Deb, you and 'J' will cover me. Tonya, you, Crissy, and Tiny will cover the rally. Now remember, no matter what you hear or see, do not leave Waters alone."

"You know, Daddy, there's going to be hundreds of people at the rally. We'll be alone out there," Tynisha said.

"That means you, Deb, and 'J' will be on your own with a trio of women who are suffering from low sex drive," Christina interjected with a grin.

"We'll be okay, little girl," Derrick said, smiling at his girls, reassuring them everything would go alright.

Tonya looked at her girls, including Debra; smiling, she asked, "Did the departments know what they were getting when you four joined the forces?"

"Hell, no! But it's too damn late for that now, ain't it?" snorted Debra.

Tonya shook her head and smiled, as did her sisters and Derrick.

"Come on, you clowns, let's go; we don't want to keep Waters waiting," Derrick said, staring at Debra.

Puzzled, Debra asked, "What? Well, hell, they didn't."

Derrick said nothing, simply smiled.

"Does everyone have on their vest, and have their walkie-talkies?" Tonya asked.

"Got them," Tynisha said, as did everyone else walking out the door.

• • • •

"I'm not going to stand here and tell you that I will be the best mayor this city will ever have. You, the citizens of Philadelphia, already know that I'm the best man for the next eight years."

"How long do we have to stay here with old motor mouth?"

"Crissy, you know what Daddy said."

"I'm not talking about leaving him, Tiny. I'm just asking how long does this rally last?"

"Crissy, it ends at five; we have twenty-five minutes left."

"Twenty-five minutes? Twenty-five minutes?" Christina repeated herself.

"Crissy, 'J'…stay off the walkie-talkies unless there is something worthwhile to talk about," Tonya's voice crackled over the walkie-talkie.

"It's Crissy, Mom, she's bored. Let me tell you something, Mom. When this girl gets bored, she gets restless. When she gets restless, she gets into trouble."

"Okay, okay," Tonya responded. "What can we do about it?"

"I want to switch places with Tiny. Tiny, switch places with me, please? Pretty please?" Christina begged her sister.

"Alright, alright! I'll do just about anything to keep you quiet. It's okay, right, Mom?"

"Fine, just to keep you two quiet."

"Crissy, there's two thousand people out here. By the time you two push through the crowd, the rally will be over. Hold it, Mom; Crissy stay where you are for right now."

"Why? What's wrong?" Christina asked in a serious tone of voice.

"Nothing, I just want to check out some movement over here on the south side. I'll be at South Broad Street Circle; I'm taking a uniform with me, so you won't have to worry. Talk to you in ten, out."

"Tiny! Tiny? Come in, Tiny. Tiny answer me, dammit," Christina demanded of her oldest sister."

"Shut up, girl. Mom?"

"Yes, I'm here, Tiny; what's wrong?"

"I'm not sure, but I thought there wasn't any parking around here until after the rally."

"Yeah, so what?" Christina asked.

"So, there's a big black van parked here with false police decals and markings on it."

"Don't go near that van, Tynisha, do you hear me? Do not go near that van!" Tonya screamed over the walkie-talkie.

"Okay, Mom, I'll wait for you to get here, but hurry."

"I'm coming, too," Christina told her sister.

"No! You stay put!" Tonya commanded.

"Like hell, I will. Sorry, Mom, but I've already lost one sister, I am not about to lose another."

"Understood, Crissy, I'll meet you there. We're on our way, baby."

"Hurry up you two," Tynisha pleaded.

Justina walked over to her father, who was sitting on a park bench, drinking bottled water. Derrick was sitting in Love Park, a city-owned public park two blocks west of City Hall. During the hot, sweltering days of summer, children came to splash and play in the fountain to cool off. A place where lovers came to sit and talk, the park was also host to the many people who came there to eat their noontime meals. Until the City passed a law forbidding the practice, the homeless slept on the benches day and night.

"I don't think he is coming, Daddy," Justina told her father.

"Let's give him a few more minutes, he'll be here," Derrick assured his daughter.

"Dad, we've been waiting here for two hours, you said that Mr. Taurus has never been late for anything. There's something wrong, Dad; something isn't right, I don't like this."

"You feel it, too?" Derrick asked.

"Besides, Daddy, you don't need to be out here in this air like this. It's a little nippy," Justina complained.

"It feels good to me, little girl."

"Yeah right, Daddy. Daddy? What are you going to do about Shannon since Mom has come back? Are you going to break off the relationship or what?"

"Whoa, little girl, slow down... Oh, my god! Debra," Derrick started running toward his adopted daughter, who was walking toward him and Justina in a trance-like state.

"Debbie!"" Justina screamed when she spotted her sister. "No! No, dear God, no! Not again, please!"

Derrick reached Debra and noticed she was in partial shock. Derrick panicked when he saw that the white and blue windbreaker jacket she was wearing was splattered with blood. "Where are you hit?" Derrick yelled at her, while ripping open her jacket.

She stared up at her father and said, "It's not my blood, Daddy."

"What?"

"It's not my blood."

Derrick ripped open her blouse. She had on her bulletproof vest. "Good girl," Derrick said as he turned Debra around, checking her head, neck, and back for a point of entry or exit...none.

"It's not my blood, Daddy," Debra again repeated herself.

Derrick started walking her toward the bench where he and Justina were sitting.

Justina yelled, "Daddy!"

"She's not hit 'J', she's not hit."

Justina grabbed her sister and held her tight.

"I'm alright, I'm okay," said Debra.

Derrick sat Debra down on the bench. "Debra? Since this isn't your blood, then whose blood is it?"

"His," Debra answered, as she handed her father a calling card.

Derrick took the blood-splattered card and wiped it off on the arm of his light baby blue jacket sleeve. The card read, TAURUS THE BULL. "Oh, my god! The girls! Your mother! 'J', get her to the car and stay with her, I've got to find your mom and your sisters." Derrick started running east toward City Hall.

Christina reached the south side of Broad Street Circle before Tonya did; she started looking around for her sister and the van. Panic started to rumble in her stomach. Christina spotted a black-uniformed female officer and ran over to her. Pulling out her badge, she identified herself and asked her if she had seen Tynisha or the van. The officer stated to her that she spotted Tynisha looking the van over. She said she started toward the van when a black male, uniformed cop started talking to her sister, then they both walked to the back of the van. The officer said by the time she pushed her way thru the crowd and was about fifty feet from the van, it took off. Both the uniformed cop and Tynisha were gone.

Christina sat on the curb and mumbled to herself, "They got my sister, they took my sister."

"Crissy? Crissy?" Christina heard her mother's voice.

Christina stood and spotted Tonya walking away from her. "Over here, Mom, over here!" Christina shouted.

Tonya turned around, saw her daughter, and ran over to her. "Where is Tiny? Crissy, where is your sister?" Tonya shook Christina, "Have you found your sister?"

"They took her!" Christina yelled at her mother.

"Took her? Who took her? Took her where?"

"You tell me, they're your friends," Christina snapped at her mother.

•　　•　　•　　•

"They won't kill her, Centaur," Aquarius assured Derrick. "They are making sure that they have an ace to play when it's time for them to get out of the city." Derrick said nothing.

"Are you alright, Deb?" Angel asked her cousin.

"Yes, I'm just fine, I think. I'm just wondering what's up with me and blood all of a sudden... first dog blood, now human blood. What am I, a goddamn vampire?"

Tonya cracked a half smile.

"Our only chance to get Tiny back is on Election Day," Derrick speculated.

"How do you figure, Daddy?" Justina asked.

"Each of them will be at their appointed station; they will have to leave Tiny at wherever they are. It will be too much for them to drag her along with them," Derrick answered.

"I want to know why the hell they killed Mr. Taurus," Debra asked.

"Taurus was dead set against kidnapping. The first time it was mentioned, kidnapping one of you ladies, he bluntly, straight out said 'no'," Aquarius finished.

"Seems like one of them liked the idea, but which one?" Debra asked.

'Your Aunt Teresa. She liked the idea from the start, but she wanted to go a step farther. Teresa wanted to kidnap all four sisters, one at a time."

"Why one at a time?" Derrick wanted to know.

"Wouldn't have any choice. They would have been a handful one at a time; who in their right state of mind would try to kidnap all four of them at once?

Then take this into consideration, we didn't have any idea about Debra. That way Derrick wouldn't have had any choice but to back off. We talked about it behind Taurus's back. I was for taking one of the sisters, but not all four—that, I was against. Scorpio said 'no', and your mother warned all of us, including your aunt, to stay away from her kids. She told Cancer, after Cancer told her she would have no qualms about hurting or killing one or all the girls if any or all got into the way. She warned Cancer that if she so much as touched or harmed any one of you, she would kill her. I also know why Teresa suggested all four of you."

"Why?" Tonya asked.

"To keep them alive and safe. She knew if we had all four girls, Derrick would've been too busy looking for them to protect Waters. Waters would've been an easy kill…in and out. But after my wife and your daughter were killed, that plan was shot to hell. Taurus didn't want any further part of the remaining three. Actually, he was looking forward to seeing his god kids. He loved and missed those girls is what he told me in private," Aquarius finished.

"He was standing right next to me. He was carrying three large gift-wrapped packages. We were waiting for the light to change to cross J.F.K. Boulevard when he dropped the packages and grabbed his throat. That's when the second shot hit him in the forehead and he fell backwards and hit the ground. When I checked for vital signs, he was already dead. That's when I saw the calling card sticking halfway out of his pocket," Debra said, recalling the incident.

"I'm willing to bet that those packages were for you three ladies," Aquarius said.

"Mom, I didn't mean to say…"

"Shh… It's alright, baby; it's okay," Tonya interrupted Christina.

"What do we do now?" Debra asked.

"We wait, we wait for Election Day, then we end this madness," Derrick answered.

•   •   •   •

Tynisha just sat and stared at her captors, counting them to herself in her head. *One, Ms. Libra; two, Ms. Cancer; three, Aunt Teresa;* the fourth and fifth she had never seen before. *The fourth must be Ms. Aries* she deduced. So, who were the two men looking at her? *Mr. Leo? Mr. Virgo or Mr. Taurus? It really doesn't matter. Daddy is going to kill them all for kidnapping me and for killing my baby sister.*

"Take the gag and the leg shackles off, that's no way to treat our guest of honor," a man ordered as he entered the room.

"But, Leo!" Cancer started to protest.

"No buts, take them off; she's a trained police officer, she won't be a problem. Besides, she's still chained by the waist."

Cancer stood and walked over to Tynisha, and untied the scarf wrapped around her mouth. "Now go ahead and scream so I can knock your ass out."

Tynisha said nothing, as Cancer took the leg shackles off. Tynisha sighed with relief. The leg irons were on too tight.

"You see? No problem at all. Hi, Tynisha, I'm Leo. That's Virgo." Virgo nodded his head. "This is Aries."

"Hello, Tynisha."

"Hello, Ms. Aries," Tynisha responded.

"Hmm, polite and have manners, too; I like that," Aries said smiling. "You already know...."

"Who, the three bitches of Eastwick?" Tynisha cut Leo off.

Leo, Virgo, and Aries smirked. "Well, your niece does know you, Teresa," Virgo instigated.

Teresa smiled, walked over to Tynisha, and slapped her hard across the right side of her face. The force of the slap was hard enough to split the corner of her right upper and lower lips.

"Teresa!" Leo shouted.

"Watch your tongue, young lady. I'm still your aunt and you will respect me," she screamed in Tynisha's face.

Tynisha spats the blood built up in her mouth into her aunt's face. "Fuck you, bitch, you ain't shit to me," Tynisha yelled. Tynisha felt the blunt pain in her right temple; she gave out a low moan then everything went black.

Aries grabbed Teresa by the left arm, spinning her around, and gave her a back-hand slap. The blow sent her to the floor. Teresa, reeling from the blow, felt and tasted the blood coming from her nose and her mouth.

"I going to kill you, bitch," Teresa screamed at Aries.

"Stay there," Aries warned the now demented woman.

Teresa picked herself off the floor and charged Aries, screaming, "I'm going to kill you."

Aries waited until the charging, mad woman reached five feet from her, took one step forward, and delivered a ferocious forward kick to her forehead, knocking Teresa unconscious. Teresa fell lifeless to the floor.

"Goddamn," Virgo exclaimed.

"Holy shit, is she dead?" Cancer asked.

"What the hell is wrong with you, Aries?" Leo shouted.

"No! Leo, what the hell is wrong with her? If she is going to hit somebody, let it be somebody who can defend himself or herself, not someone who is shackled to a chair against a wall."

"Man! Is that bitch gonna have a bad headache when she wakes up; not even considering the fact she is going to be pissed off, too," grinned Libra.

"It's not funny, Libra," Leo growled.

"It's a damn good thing Aries had on sneakers instead of those boots she normally wears, otherwise, she wouldn't have a head on her shoulders," Cancer laughed.

"Pick her up and sit her on a chair and cuff her hands behind her back; we'll let her loose after she cools down; help him, Aries, you put her there," Leo commanded.

"Fuck her."

"Help him," Leo demanded.

"No, Leo, first she tries to kill her and then she demands respect from her, that's bullshit and you know it. Let the whore stay there," Aries protested.

"I'll help you, Vir," Cancer said, still laughing. Aries left the room.

"Now, where is she going?" Leo asked.

A few minutes passed before Aries returned with an ice pack, a glass of water, and two pills. Aries applied the ice pack to Tynisha's temple.

Tynisha started to stir; she started to lift her head, then stopped, as the pain started to register to her brain. "Ooh, it hurts," Tynisha complained.

"Take these, Tynisha, it will ease your headache," Aries told her.

Tynisha lifted her head and Aries put the pills in her mouth, holding the glass of water to her lips. "Thank you, Ms. Aries."

"You're welcome, kid, you're welcome."

Tynisha then lifted her head and spotted her aunt knocked out cold; she then noticed the black and blue mark on her forehead. Tynisha looks at Aries and smiled. Aries returned the smile, while shrugging her shoulders.

"Here young lady, call your father and let him know that you are alright," Leo demanded, handing Tynisha a cell phone.

"No!" Tynisha responded. "I want him mad enough to kill you on sight."

"If you want to live long enough to see that happen, you'll make the call."

"I said no," Tynisha rebelled. "You can kill me if you want to; you killed my baby sister, what's the difference? I'm no better than she was, so go ahead, do your worst."

"Please, do it for me, Tynisha, please," Aries pleaded. "You do not want to suffer the kind of pain Leo can dish out; trust me, you don't."

Tynisha looked at Aries for a minute. Then after looking at her aunt sleeping in the chair, she gave in. "I'm doing this because of you, Ms. Aries, not because he demanded I do it." Tynisha snatched the phone from Leo.

The phone rang once. "Hello, Four Sisters..."

"Hi, Patty, it's me Tiny; put Daddy on the line, please."

"Hold on, Tynisha, I'll go get him, hold on." Patty ran into Tynisha's room. "Boss, it's Tiny."

Derrick pushed a button on the intercom phone so all could hear. "I'm here, baby."

"Hi, Daddy."

"Are you alright, baby?"

"Yes, I'm alright for now, Daddy; besides a headache, a love you gift from Aunt Teresa."

"Are you sure, sweetheart?"

"Yes, Daddy, I'm fine..."

"Don't bother with trying to trace the call, Centaur; it won't work, the signal is scrambled."

"Ms. Libra," Justina yelled.

"Is that you, Justina? How are you, girlfriend? Can't wait to beat your stupid ass silly."

"Hello, Debra?" Hey, I haven't met you, yet, but my name is Aries. Can't wait to kill you...er...meet you."

"Oh, Christina, your aunt would have loved to speak to you, but right now she's out of it."

"Hey, traitor, see you soon," Virgo laughed.

"Count on it," Aquarius replied.

"Hey Tonya, Miss Tracy? Don't worry; you'll be joining her soon, real soon."

"Cancer, I'm going to rip your eyes out of your head!" Tonya screamed at the phone.

"Your kid has a nasty temper, Centaur, reminds me of you."

"Leo?"

"Hello, Centaur, how are you?"

"I'm fine, Leo, and you?"

"I'm making it for a middle age man. Nothing is going to happen to your kid as long as she behaves herself. I give you my word, Centaur, your child minds her manners and she will come out of this without a scratch, trust me."

"Can I do that, Leo? Can I trust you?"

"You'll find out on Election night. Until then, don't forget to vote." Leo hung up the phone.

"They are going to kill my sister," Christina said, starting to cry.

"No, Crissy, no they are not going to kill her. If they were, she would be dead already," Derrick reassured Christina. "Tonya? Do the Correctors know about the Club?"

"Yes, they do, there is some club information in your file; why you ask?"

"I don't think it's safe being here any longer; we've got to move. Listen up, everyone," Derrick said. "Tomorrow we'll be moving to the Chestnut Hill resident for safety reasons. Aquarius, you are welcome to stay there, too, we have plenty of room, and we will feel better if you do."

"Thank you, Centaur, I think I will take you up on that offer."

"Oh, no you're not. Not without me, you're not," Angel spoke up.

"Angel, calm down. We knew from the start that you were not going to let him out of your sight."

"Angel? I just know you are not getting loud with my dad, are you?" Justina asked with a big grin on her face."

"Hey, 'J' I'll get loud with your ass," Angel said smiling.

"Oh, that's how you going to act? Dad, give me Bonnie's phone number, I'll stop Ms. Sassy-Behind right here and now." Everyone burst out in laughter, including Angel.

"The hell with you 'J'," Angel said laughing.

"Then it's settled, we move out tomorrow morning after breakfast," Derrick said, shaking his head, and mumbling, "You kids are crazy."

• • • •

The next day:

"Oh hell, we've got problems," Virgo said, looking out the front room window past the white shade.

"What's up?" Leo asked.

"Look outside and see," Virgo replied.

Leo looked out the window to see two police officers looking in the passenger and driver side window. "Why the hell are they checking out our car?"

"Because it's parked in front of a fire hydrant, that's why," Aries said, coming into the room carrying two bags of grocery.

"Man, we still have some C-4 in the trunk of that car," Virgo complained.

"We have to get the hell out of here," Aries advised.

"Wait a minute; we may not have to leave. They don't know who owns that car. As long as they don't find out whose car it is, we're safe," Virgo replied, walking away from the window.

"Damn, wishful thinking," Leo grunted.

"That old lady across the street on the second floor, well she just came out of her building to talk to the cops. I told you, you should have let me kill that old bitty the first time I found her spying on us," Cancer complained.

"Oh shit, now what?" Virgo asked.

"That old bitty, as Cancer calls her, is pointing at our house," Leo responded. "It's time to go, people; the cops are getting on their radios. Let's move it out the back door," Leo ordered. We have about ten minutes before this street is full of cops."

"Damn! And we haven't even eaten breakfast yet," Teresa complained.

"Come on or you will have a lifetime of eating breakfast in the slammer, providing they don't give you a lethal injection," Leo remarked.

"What about my niece?" Teresa asked.

"Kill her," Cancer responded with a smile.

"No!" Leo shouted at Cancer. "You are one sick sister. Leave her here. Gag her and put the shackles back on," he ordered Aries and Teresa. "We'll put your bags in the car."

Aries placed the gag back around Tynisha's mouth. "Sorry, honey, but I have to do this for our sake, you do understand, don't you?"

"Yes, I understand," Tynisha answered.

"Ms. Aries?"

"Yes, Tynisha?"

"Thank you, I'll make sure that my mom, my dad, or my sisters don't kill you when this is all over."

Looking at Teresa with fire in her eyes, Tynisha said, "I can't wait."

"Neither can I, you little nappy-headed Sambo," Teresa laughed, as she put the shackles back on Tynisha's legs, too tight. "I'll deal with your black ass when we get back to LA," Teresa told Aries with a snarl.

"Ooh, I can't wait," Aries said smiling. Aries started walking to the door of the room, when she turned around in time to see Teresa punch Tynisha on the right side of her head. "You are fucked-up in the head, you know that?" Aries yelled at Teresa.

"I did that so she wouldn't make any noises."

Tynisha gave out a low moan as she passed out.

"Bitch," Aries said, as she walked out of the room. Teresa laughed.

Ten minutes passed before the SWAT team shot tear gas through the front windows at the now almost empty room where Tynisha sat unconscious. The SWAT team had been demanding that the occupants of the row house come out with their hands up. When there was no response, they decided to use tear gas canisters before storming the house. After five minutes of no movement or sound, they decided to raid the building. The first two officers who entered the house found Tynisha gagging on her own vomit. "Over here, we've found one," one officer yelled out the window. The officer yelled, Get a medic in here fast," as he ripped the gag off Tynisha's mouth.

Tynisha released the backed up vomit. The officer proceeded to uncuff her hands. The officer had to catch Tynisha as she slumped forward. When the second officer approached Tynisha, as other SWAT team members invaded the rest of the building, he screamed out, "Oh my god, Tiny?" It was David, Tynisha's fiancé. "Oh my god, baby, we are going to take care of you. You are going to be okay, baby. Hold on, help is coming, "Medic," David shouted as a fire department medic with a gas mask on approached her. Again, Tynisha passed out.

• • • •

One hour later:

The Correctors had just finished moving into their new headquarters, when Libra announced, "They are on the move. Should we surprise them now and get this thing over with?" Virgo asked.

"No, no yet," Leo said. "Libra, go follow them; find out where they are going. It's safe to say they haven't heard from Tynisha yet, so we can use the opportunity to get them out of our hair once and for all. Libra?"

"Yeah, Leo?"

"Like I always said, you don't talk much, but when you have something to say, it always makes sense. Brilliant, that's all I can say, brilliant. I never would've thought of moving across the street from the Four Sisters' Club. I mean, who would have the balls to even suggest it," Leo laughed as Libra walked to the stairs of the second floor of the three-story building. "Don't get too close, you don't want to be spotted."

"Okay, Leo," Libra said, going down the steps.

• • • •

The beginning of the END:

"Daddy, how long has it been since we moved out of this old house?" Christina asked Derrick.

"Almost twenty years. We moved here when Tracy was two," Derrick answered, as he tried to hold back the tears.

"Sorry, Daddy; didn't mean to bring back old memories."

"It's okay, baby."

The Jenkins and company never noticed the white car parked halfway down the street with Libra sitting, watching as they entered the old ranch-style house in the high-class neighborhood. Rosa, who was the last one to arrive, noticed the car and it's occupant as she drove past. Rosa drove her black car around the block so she could get a better look at the driver. Many of the wealthy homeowners in the neat tree-lined, private complex had maids, cooks, and butlers, and she knew every one of them. By it being ten o'clock in the morning, Rosa knew that all the hired hands in the area would already be in the houses of their employer.

This woman was a stranger, and she had a funny feeling that she was trouble. Libra didn't pay much attention when the car parked in front of her in the open space. Rosa exited the vehicle and nodded a greeting with a smile to Libra. Libra nodded her head in return. Rosa walked the forty yards or more to the Jenkins's residence.

•　　•　　•　　•

It was three o'clock when the mayor called Derrick to inform him and his family that Tynisha had been found alive.

"Would you hold on a second, Mr. Mayor, while I put the phone on intercom?"

"Go ahead, Derrick."

Derrick pushed the intercom button, so the rest of the group could hear. "Go ahead, sir."

"Tynisha was found in a house in Society Hill about nine-fifteen this morning. She is in good condition, recovering from a concussion, and being exposed to tear gas. She's at Social Hospital; she's still in the emergency ward. She's beat up a bit, but she is in good spirits. It seems that you and Tonya's friends are gypsies. They don't stay in one place very long, do they?"

"Never did, Your Honor," Tonya answered.

"Who is Teresa, Tonya?" the mayor asked.

Tonya looked at Derrick, who nodded his head, indicating for her to tell the mayor. "She's my sister, Your Honor."

"Well, I'm sorry about that, Tonya. When I catch up with her, I'm going to put a bullet in her black ass for what she did to my godchild. Tynisha is under heavy guard, Derrick. The word is spreading throughout the department about Tynisha. Derrick, Tonya, if any one on the force catches one or all of the Correctors, they will shoot first, ask questions later. Commanders of every district have given their people orders of shoot to kill. They are no longer interested in bringing them in, and they are not taking any chances. It's bad enough what happened last month, but to kidnap and torture one of their own? The men and women in blue are pissed."

"Torture, Your Honor?"

"Yes, it seems like your sister got great delight in punching Tynisha in the right temple, knocking her out each time she did it."

"I'm going to beat that bitch lifeless," Christina screamed. "So help me God, I am going to kill her and God have mercy on both our souls," Christina said crying.

"Your Honor, we are on our way to the hospital."

"I'm still here; I will see you when you get here."

"Good, we'll see you in about an hour." Derrick hung up the phone. Twenty-five minutes later, Derrick was asking everyone if they had their weapons, and bulletproof vests on. "Angel, you and Aquarius stay put. We do not want to have to answer a bunch of questions that we can't or don't want to answer."

"What? I can't go and see my cousin? What kind of shit is that?" Angel asked in protest.

"No!" Derrick answered in a sharp tone of voice. "Not now, you can go later on. Besides, you and Aquarius are our last line of defense. If those fools decide to ambush us..."

Derrick was interrupted by the sound of the double barrel shotgun blast ripping through the maple wood front door. Derrick was hit in the chest and knocked backwards into the iron step railing, hitting his head, knocking him out. The second blast sent Angel to the floor, with the small pellets lodging into her left side and hip.

"Daddy!" Christina shouted as she dove to the floor behind the white L-shaped living room sofa, pulling out her 9-mm weapon as she hit the floor.

"Angel!" Aquarius cried out, as he pulled out his black 9-mm weapon.

Leo stood on the outside of the splintered door, still firing the shotgun. Six of the front bay windows shattered from the .45-caliber, semi-automatic bullets being fired from three different directions. Aries was firing from the left side of the front bay window, Libra was firing from the right side, and Cancer is in the middle, firing in the living room.

"Mom! Look out!" Debra screamed as Cancer aimed her weapon from outside of the broken window frame, then fired once, then a second time.

The first projectile hit Tonya in the right shoulder; she screamed out in pain, as the impact knocked her over a round, brown leather ottoman, sitting in front of a brown leather easy chair. The second missed her head, as she fell backward. Tonya hit her head as she hit the carpeted floor, and passed out.

Debra returned fire, as she took cover behind a 52-inch television.

Cancer smiling, satisfied she hit Tonya, took cover behind the outside wall, out of the line of fire.

Aquarius, with caution, crawled over to Angel, who was lying on the floor, bleeding heavily from the hip wound.

"Get out of here!" she yelled at Aquarius. "Please go, don't let them catch you. You know they will kill you on sight," Angel pleaded with her lover.

"No, I'm not leaving you, Angel. Aquarius did not notice Virgo coming up behind him.

Angel screamed out, "No!" as the bullet hit Aquarius in the left shoulder blade. Aquarius fell flat on top of Angel.

Virgo smiled as he took aim at Aquarius's head and said, "Goodbye, my one-time friend."

"Excuse me," Virgo heard a female voice behind him.

Virgo turned around to see Rosa standing in front of him with a .357 Magnum in her hand. "I didn't want to shoot you in the back. I'm not a coward like you," Rosa said, as she pulled the trigger. The impact sent Virgo five feet across the room into a wall partition separating the living room from a small walk-in closet. Virgo went into shock, as the bullet hit him in the heart. "Now, please die," Rosa asked, as Virgo slid to the floor dead. "Thank you," Rosa said, making the sign of the cross on her chest.

"Let's get out of here," Leo shouted to the rest of the Correctors, as he heard police sirens in the background.

"Wait, I have dessert. I hope you like pineapple," Cancer said, as she threw a hand grenade through the front window. The explosion ripped apart the silence of the afternoon tranquility.

•　　•　　•　　•

Tynisha, who had been placed into a room, heard the 'officers down, assist' call over David's radio. David a 6' even, 245–pound, twenty-nine year old, part

Irish, part Italian, six-year member of Philadelphia's SWAT team unit. Normally a quiet man, he had a bad temper when it came down to the safety and welfare of Tynisha.

David met Tynisha when she came into the Academy. The two hit it off from the beginning. They both took some ribbing from their families when they told them of each other's race, but to their shock, their families blessed their union with love and warmth. David was the youngest of nine siblings—four sisters and five brothers—all police officers. His father was a retired police captain, who has worked with Derrick and knew him very well.

David turned off the radio with hopes that his fiancée did not hear the transmission. No such luck. "Turn the TV on," Tynisha asked David.

"Honey, I don't think this is the right time to be watching TV."

"Too late, David, turn it on or I will get up and do it myself."

Not wanting to further upset his future wife, he turned on the television. "Police are still converging on the scene as we speak. Again, we are at the scene of a deadly gun battle, coming to a climax with a hand grenade being tossed into the house. So far, there are reports of one man dead, two wounded, and two women also wounded in this terrible melee. Police refuse to confirm or deny that the victims of this assault are the Jenkins family. Sources say that Derrick Jenkins, a retired inspector of the Philadelphia Police and his former wife, daughters, and some friends came under attack about thirty minutes ago. Neighbors report that there were no less than two hundred shots fired into the Jenkins's family home. As you can see behind me, there are about ten rescue wagons and about four fire company trucks here to assist. G.W.P. is also here to make sure that there is no chance of gas exploding in the residence. I estimate that there are about one hundred police officers on the scene. You will remember, Derrick Jenkins lost his youngest daughter when someone blew up the EFO oil refinery, where a number of police and firemen were killed, including Tracy Jenkins in her rookie year on the police force. Not even to mention the citizens killed when one of the burning police cars flew into a one-family residence, killing all five occupants."

"No!" Tynisha screamed.

Two police officers rushed into the room. David, sitting on the bed holding the now shaken and crying woman, told the two officers, "Someone just attacked her family. Turn off that damn television, please!"

• • • •

Five days later, Sunday, November 5, the Jenkins's Roxborough residence...THE FINAL CLASH:

"How are you feeling, Ms. Debra?" Rosa asked.

"This is the very last time I'm going to tell you, Rosa; my name is Debra or Deb, okay?"

"Okay, Ms. Debra," Rosa answered with a smile.

"I'm feeling a little better, where's 'J'?"

"She's upstairs in your parents' room, still crying," Rosa answered, leaving the den.

"Rosa? Just what the hell are we going to do now? Dad is dead; Mom is lying in the hospital with a hole in her shoulder and a broken collarbone. Tynisha is still in the hospital in shock, and on top of that, both Angel and Aquarius are in the hospital, recovering from their wounds. It's just me, Crissy, and 'J' left. How can just the three of us take on those maniacs and protect Waters at the same time? How, Rosa?"

"The Lord will provide, Ms. Debra, have faith. He will provide."

"They really brought it to us and we were careful."

Christina, who was lying on the sofa, got up and hugged her crying sister. "It's not over, yet. Have faith, we are going to come out on top. We are not beaten, just yet. We aren't beaten until we are dead."

"Damn right, little sister."

"We are Jenkins. Take down one, two more spring up."

"Huh? Who?" Debra turned her head toward the sound of the woman's voice.

"Gail? Greta? Oh, my god!" Christina screamed, running to her two oldest sisters. Gail snatches her younger sister and gave her a firm, warm bear hug.

Christina broke out in a serious cry.

"Go ahead, lil sister, get it all out of your system. After what all of you have been through, you deserve it. And, you must be Debra, our newest addition to the family. Come and give your sister a hug." Greta held out her arms, as Debra reached Greta and wrapped her arms around her waist and she, too, broke down in an earnest cry.

After Christina let go of Gail, she hugged Greta and Gail hugged Debra. After the exchange of greetings, the four women sat down in the den to talk about what's been happening over the last seven weeks.

"Crissy, why didn't you tell me you have two older sisters?"

"Would you believe I forgot?"

"Hell no!"

"Besides, I thought Daddy told you."

"You mean why didn't she tell you that you have two older sisters, don't you?" Gail asked.

"Yeah," Debra smiled.

"Listen, Deb, we'll give you the scoop on all of that after we clean up this bullshit. But right now, I'm going upstairs to see Jay-Jay."

"What did I tell you about that Jay-Jay shit? This is not a good time to come in here messing up my name. My name is Justina or 'J', I'll kick your ass," Justina said with a big, warm smile on her face, as she walked down the steps leading to the den.

"You wish, hussy," Gail said, as she stood up to greet her now youngest sister. There were a few moments of silence, as Justina hugged and kissed both of her sisters on the cheeks.

After all the greetings were over, Rosa came into the den to announce that lunch was now being served. "And, you will eat your vegetables, Ms. Gail, and no buts," Rosa said with a smile on her face.

"Yes, Ma'am," Gail mumbled in a low tone. Everyone laughed.

After the women finished eating and Rosa had cleared the table, she asked if there was anything else.

"No, and thank you, Rosa," Gail answered.

"Rosa? Take the rest of the week off. If anyone of us deserves it, it's you," Justina said.

"Thank you, Ms. Justina, but I have been taking care of you young ladies since you've been little. My job is to watch over you and watch over you, I will."

"But, Rosa, we are grown now," Christina said.

"Ms. Christina, you were grown when you were little. I took care of you then, and I take care of you now."

Christina and her sisters burst out in laughter. "I give up. Rosa, there's no beating you," Christina said through her laughter. Rosa left the den.

"Okay, I have something to tell you three," Gail started off the discussion. First of all, Daddy's not dead. But...let me get this all out before you start asking questions," Gail interrupted Debra. "Daddy, Mom, Angel, and Aquarius are all in Hawaii. They were flown there yesterday at my and Greta's request. Daddy had on his bulletproof vest when he was shot. It's a good thing it was a chest hit, or Daddy would have been killed. However, he did suffer a nasty heart attack. He's on life support right now, but only to help him breath. Daddy's heart took a lot of stress, but the doctors told us he should recover. As for Mom, she is in good condition. She pretty much took a beating when that bullet hit her, but she, too, is doing fine. The FBI is not happy, neither is the secret service."

"What the hell does the secret service have to do with this?" Christina asked.

"It seems like your friends who tried to off you, are into making funny money and using it to finance killing high-level drug dealers."

"Hell, that's a plus on their behalf," Justina said frowning.

"Angel, Angel is in good condition. She had on her vest, too, but she took a lot of pellets into her left hip. She won't be able to walk for a while, but she, too, will recover. The one you call Aquarius, he remains in poor condition. He's in the hospital with a bullet wound in the back. The bullet exploded on impact and it shredded different parts of his back. A few pieces of shrapnel hit his right lung, but he, too, will make it with a lot of tender loving care."

"I'm quite sure Angel will provide that," Justina said smiling.

"If it wasn't for Rosa killing the one you called Virgo, Aquarius would be dead."

"Chalk up one for the good guys," Debra said, with a gleeful look in her eyes. "Gail?"

"Yes, Debra?"

"You mentioned everyone but Tiny, what happened to her? Where is she? Is she alright? Please don't tell me Tiny is dead." Panic started to settle in the three women's hearts.

"Slow down, little sis, slow down. Ask her yourself."

Tynisha entered the den with a big smile on her face. Debra, Christina, and Justina jumped up from the sofa and ran to their sister, knocking her down.

• • • •

"Okay, Mr. Smart Ass, now what do we do?" Cancer asked Leo.

"What are you talking about? We do what we came here to do," Leo answered, annoyed.

"Just like that? Just like that? How in the hell are we going to kill Waters now? I don't know if you noticed, but we are down to five members, five!" shouted Cancer.

"We need some help, and we need it bad," Aries stated. "The election is two days away. We just lost Virgo, and on top of that, we don't have any information on any of the Jenkins girls. Tynisha was released from the hospital, Derrick is dead, we don't know if Tonya is dead or alive, and we don't know anything, anything," Aries continued. "And, what about Aquarius? Virgo put a bullet in his back before being killed by the maid, the fucking maid for Christ's sake."

"Aquarius's girlfriend was hit, too!" Cancer yelled at Leo.

"You know something? We can't even get within one hundred feet of the hospitals that they are in because of all of the cops that are there. I was watching television when they announced Derrick's death; he's being buried in Florida. What's going to happen next?" Aries asked Leo.

"I'll tell you what's going to happen," Gemini spoke up. "My nieces are mourning the death of their father, for one; for two, their mother was shot; and three, Leo shot the woman that was with Aquarius. Tell me, what the hell do you think is going to happen? Those three women are going to hunt us down and kill all five of us. That's what's going to happen next," Gemini politely explained. "Forget any rules and regulations, that shit is down the drain. When those three catch up with you, Leo, only God will be able to identify your remains, I bullshit you not," Gemini ended her remarks.

"Leo, we need some help, plain and simple; we need some more people if we are going to do this job and do it right," Aries snapped.

"Listen up, people. For one thing, by the time we get some more people, we won't be able to get them up to par in time for the job. Secondly, all of you are upset behind Virgo's death. We are going to do what we came here to do and nothing is going to prevent us from doing it."

"My question is how? How are we going to cover our stations and leave the others open?" Aries asked.

"We'll think of something," Leo answered.

"Leo's right, it is too late to get some help; besides, we really don't need any more help," Gemini said.

"All we have to do is cover the last five stations closest to the take-down area. If he doesn't come one way, he will come the other. I say we put him down at the high school. This way, if one of us isn't able to put him down, the other will," Libra said. "All we have to do is position ourselves at different locations in the school; he's bound to show up after the election."

"What makes you so sure that he will come to that school after the election?" Gemini asked.

"The son of a bitch is arrogant. He already announced that he would give his acceptance speech at the high school that he graduated from," Libra answered with a smile.

•　　•　　•　　•

"Tell me something. How did you two know about what was going on here? Hell, for that matter, exactly where the hell did you two come from? I mean your names were never mentioned, and I do mean not once," Debra asks.

"Okay, little sisters, let me tell you. Like you, Deb, we are adopted. Daddy picked us up off the streets. We were hookers, the both of us. Daddy was a beat cop when he first got on the force. One night Daddy was working on the strip, he spotted me and Greta getting our ass beat by our pimp. I was fourteen, Greta was thirteen years old. Daddy grabbed the pimp and started beating his ass like he was beating ours. Daddy called for a wagon and the pimp got locked up. After the pimp's trial was over, by the way, he got fourteen years for rape and about eight other charges. But anyway, the judge was about to send us to a home for wayward girls. I thought it was all over for us, but Daddy asked the judge to put us in his custody until he had a hearing for adoption. The judge looked at us and asked, 'Do you want and agree with Mr. Jenkins?' We jumped at the chance to be adopted, to sleep in a bed of our own, the chance to be able to eat until we got sick. We said 'yes'. The judge granted Daddy temporary custody until the hearing. But, you know there is always a but. The judge also said that if we caused Daddy one problem, just one, off to the home we went. Things went fine for the first two years with Daddy and our new little sisters. Fine until…"

Greta started grinning.

"Go ahead, tell them yourself, my little sister," Gail grinned.

"Like Gail said, everything was fine until we decided to go around to the playground with some kids Daddy had already told us not to associate with. So, we took our happy asses over to the playground and we started smoking reefer. Now do understand, this was our first, and mind you, our last time smoking reefer. Well, lo and behold, we got busted. I mean all six of us. You talk about mad. Daddy was so mad, I thought he was going to have a heart attack. The next thing we knew, we were in front of the same judge who had warned us to stay out of trouble. The judge said to us, 'Didn't I warn you two what would happen to you if you didn't behave?'

"At the same time, we said, 'Yes, Your Honor.'

"'Did you think I was joking?'

"'No, Your Honor.'

"'What are you, twins?' the judge asked us with a nasty look.

"And wouldn't you know it, we both answered at the same time, 'No, Your Honor.'

"The judge got mad. To make a long story short, after the judge finished chewing us out, he turned us over to the custody of Daddy. We drew a sigh of relief. That didn't last long, the next thing we knew, we were shipped off to a boarding school for girls. When we arrived at the school, we couldn't believe it. The school was beautiful.

"For the first week, we were shown around the grounds. The food was 'bad'. I mean that food was so good we got sick from eating so much." Gail was smiling. "The second week, we got measured for new clothes, new shoes new everything. Our rooms were big; we shared a room of our own. They gave us a computer, and all kinds of books pertaining to schoolwork. Third week, they gave us a bank account. Now in this bank account, they put twenty-five hundred dollars (not knowing it was Daddy's money), and that whole week, all we did was learn how to manage money and to balance our checking and savings accounts. The fourth week, we did what we wanted to do. We went to the movies and to two concerts. We could stay out as long as we wanted. For four weeks we had a damn ball. But…"

"Here she goes with that but again," the four sisters said all at once laughing.

"The fifth week, oh my god! You talk about a wake-up call? We caught hell. On that Monday morning, early now around four-thirty, some chick opened up our door and threw our asses out of the beds, screamed into our faces, and made us run outside in our pajamas. Now get this, it was raining, I mean it was pouring. When we got outside, there were about…maybe…two to three hundred girls out there crying and shaking because they were cold. That's when I noticed the signs all over the grounds. The sign read: WEL-COME TO THE PENNSYLVANIA GIRLS' SCHOOL OF DISCIPLI-NARY ACTION. I swear to all that's holy, those damn signs were not out there when we came in. Daddy later told us after we graduated that they put the signs up after we went to bed at the end of our fourth week. Well, for six-teen weeks, we caught hell like no other teenage girl could ever imagine. Daddy came up to see us once a week, and every week we begged him to get us out of there. He said he couldn't, it was part of the conditions to keep us.

"Now get a load of this; all the time we were training and going to school, we were working not only for our high school diploma, but also on our bach-elor's degree. Thing of it was, after the sixteen weeks of training was over, they kicked us out; kicked us out without our high school diploma. They sent us a letter and told us we could transfer our grades and credits we got at the school to the school we came from or we could come back to finish, plus stay to get our bachelor's degree, which would have taken four years. Gail and I had high grades, very high."

"What were your grades?" Christina asked.

"All *A*s, little sister, all *A*s," Greta smiled. "We went back and received our degree in criminal justice. Went to college and received our master's de-gree. We never made Daddy that mad again. Never."

"Are you two working your degrees today?" Debra asked.

"I'm with the treasury department," Greta answered.

"And I'm with the US Marshals," Gail said.

"Okay, tell us; we know you knew about Tracy, so why didn't you two come to the funeral or come to see Mom and Dad?" Justina asked.

"We were at the funeral. We saw when Mom passed out. And, as far as what took us so long to make ourselves present? We couldn't blow our cover."

"But, our baby sister was killed," Christina protested.

"True, true. The Correctors know only about you four; they have no idea that we exist. So, the way we figured, they are in for a big surprise. I have dibs on Leo; that bastard almost killed my father. His ass belongs to me," Gail said.

"Christina?"

"Yeah, Tiny?"

"Can we switch? I want Aunt Teresa for hitting me while I was hand-cuffed."

"You want it, you got it," Christina said in song, smiling.

"Thanks, I have Ms. Gemini," Tynisha said with a frown.

"Then I have Ms. Cancer," Christina said with a deadly smile on her face.

"I still have Ms. Libra," grunted Justina.

"Ms. Aries is mine," Debra said snorting.

"So, I guess I'll be the one who cleans up behind everyone else, damn," Greta pouted.

"Let's get down to business. The only chance for us to catch the Correctors is to play the game they're playing," Gail stated.

"How's that?" Justina asked.

"We already know how they captured Tiny by using a fake police van and dressing up as a police officer. Chances are, if it worked the first time, why not use it again. I believe that they will be dressed up as cops, uniformed or undercover. Either way, it's going to be hard to spot or catch them. That's where you four come in," Gail continued. "You know what these people look like, we don't. So, you four will have to be point."

"What do you mean point?" Christina asked.

"You four will have to go into that high school so you can be seen or noticed."

"What the hell are you talking about, be seen or noticed? As soon as they spot one of us, we are dead," Debra protested.

"Not necessarily correct," Greta cut in. Understand this; we all will be on location on the third floor where the principal's office is, right?"

"Okay," Tynisha answered.

"So, we break off into two teams. Tynisha, Debra, and I will cover the west side of the principal's office. You, Gail, and Christina will cover the south side. You see, everyone will have some sort of cover. So, once they spot one of you, they will either try to blend in or they will panic and start shooting. I'm willing to bet that the latter won't happen," Gail speculated.

"Bull, big sister. Those women are straight out of Loony Tunes City. They don't care who or how many people there are, if they spot one of us, someone will get killed," Debra concluded.

"Wait, just wait a minute," Tynisha came into the debate. "I understand where you two are coming from. You are betting that there will be so many people at Ida M. Pace, even if they did spot one or all of us, they wouldn't dare or couldn't fire their weapons. Because, if they did, they would take the chance of being captured or killed themselves," Tynisha finished with a smile.

"So, that means, if they do spot us, they won't have a choice but to take us on hand-to-hand. Hot damn, my luck is starting to change for the best," Debra grins with joy.

• • • •

Monday, November 6, 11 P.M., Ida M. Pace High School:
"Why do we have to spend the night here?" Cancer asked Leo.

"It's simple," Leo answered. "We have to have time to find our hit and run route. Did you take care of the guard, Aries?"

"No, Leo, Cancer got to him before I was able to."

"And?"

"He went to heaven," Cancer said smiling.

"You are one sick person," Leo growled.

"Thank you," Cancer acknowledged.

"Okay, this how we are going to do this. Aries, you will be in the background. Since you are the best shot here, you will take out Waters the first chance you get without getting caught. Gem, you keep the south hallway cleared, as much as possible. Libra, you have the west end doing the same as Gem. Cancer, you stick as close to Waters as possible. Cancer, do not attempt to take out Waters on your own. I will be on the fifth floor. After Aries does Waters, the three of you throw the smoke bombs. That will cause massive panic and the people will be too busy scrambling to get out of the way to think about Waters. After Waters is done, come straight to the stairs and come to the fifth floor."

"When do I do Waters, right after he's announced the winner or when he's making his acceptance speech?"

"When he comes out after his acceptance speech. You are going to have to find the ideal spot to hit Waters coming out of the principal's office. Leo."

"Why do we have to go to the fifth floor after Aries does Waters, won't we be trapped up there?" Gemini asked.

"Gem, it's simple. After Aries does what she has to do, everyone will be trying to get to the elevators and the stairs on both the west and east ends to go down. The fifth floor will be the safest place to be for the time being. We can take off the police throw away clothes and get rid of our weapons."

"Man, these guns cost eight hundred apiece," Cancer complained.

"You are getting paid two mill for the job, buy another one," Leo growled.

"What do we do about my nieces?" Gemini asked.

"They won't be much of a problem," Leo answered.

"What do you mean no problem?" Aries asked in shock.

"Leo, if any one of those women run into any one of us, we are going to have to shoot them or fight them."

"We sure as hell can't shoot them with all the people that will be there," Libra added.

"The only thing we can do is go one-on-one with them. The point is, if that scenario comes into play, we will be in trouble any way you play it," Libra concludes.

"And, as mad as those bitches are right now about their mother and father, not including that woman who was with Aquarius, plus Aquarius, we will have our hands full. You realize we won't have any choice but to kill them, Gem?" Leo stated.

"I'm good as dead anyway after you let Tynisha go," Gemini said. "If I run into Tynisha, I won't have any choice but to kill her or be killed," Gemini said with a look of gloom on her face.

"That goes for any of us," Leo stated.

"Don't worry about it, Gem, by the time we start all of the pandemonium, your nieces won't have time to concentrate on us, they will be too busy with Waters," Libra said with a half smile.

"I just hope you are right, Libra. I hope for all our sakes you are right," Gemini said.

"Look, there are only three of them left; Derrick is dead, Tonya and Aquarius are out of it. The woman with Aquarius was just in the wrong place at the wrong time. They know that they can't cover Waters and fight us at the same time; it's a win, win situation," Leo stated.

"These hallways are long and dark; even with the lights on, it's eerie," Aries said.

"Go and find your spots, after you find them, come back here and let me know so I can go back with you to okay it," Leo said, as the four women broke off in different directions. "Cancer! No more killing guards, understand?"

"Whatever, Leo, whatever," "Cancer answered with a sinister smile on her face. Leo shook his head as Cancer walked down the west end of the corridor.

• • • •

Tuesday, November 7, Election Day, 5:00 P.M., the Jenkins Residence in Roxborough.

"I still don't understand how we can just let Waters walk around the city without at least one of us with him," Tynisha said to Gail.

"Little sister, Waters is not in danger until at least eleven o'clock tonight when they announce the winner of the election. According to you, the contract states Waters is not to be killed until he wins, am I right?"

"Yeah, go on," Tynisha said.

"If these people are as devious as your say they are, then I bet my life they are already at the high school right now at this very moment. Okay, and if they are there at this very moment, then this is the time to smoke them out without any innocent bystanders getting in the way, getting hurt or killed," Debra said smiling.

"Smart, big sis, real smart. What floor is the principal's office on?"

"The second floor," Justina answered, "why?"

"Then that's where we are going," Greta answered.

"Right now?"

"Right now. That school is closed now, the people there now are the people who clean up the school, the ones leaving their workplaces, and the camera crews from the news stations are there, setting up for tonight. Hell, arrogant ass isn't even there; he won't be there until after he gets the results back. We can have all the doors closed and locked down while we search all the rooms and the hallways," Gail finished.

"So, we are just going to go to that high school and demand that they close it down? Yeah, right, the only thing they are going to do is to send our asses to the 7th floor of the nearest nut farm," Debra protested.

"Again, little sister, I am with the Treasury Department and Gail is a US deputy marshal; besides, your godfather is the current mayor," Gail said with a gleam in her eyes, picking up the phone and handing it to Tynisha. "Call your godfather."

Tynisha dialed the private number to the mayor. "Hello, God Dad? It's Tiny... Yes, good to hear you, too... Yes, my sisters are alright, too... Yes, including Debra... God Dad? We need for you to close down Pace High School... Why? We have reasons to believe that the Correctors are there setting up for tonight... Yes, God Dad, we know that we can't handle those maniacs on our own, that's why we have Gail and Greta here to back us up... Yes, sir, they are standing right in front of me now; Gail is the one who told me to call you... Sure you can talk to her, hold on a sec'." Tynisha handed Gail the phone.

"Hello, Unc... Yes, it's really me... Yes, I'm fine; Greta is fine, too... Yes, you can talk to her, too. Unc, what about the school?... Thank you, Unc... No, Unc, we won't get ourselves killed before we see you. Yes, speaking for Greta and me, we promise... Sure, hold on a sec'. Greta, it's for you."

Greta took the phone. Tynisha, Debra, Christina, and Justina were all looking at their two older sisters with their mouths wide open in shock.

"Okay, Unc, you take care, too... What's that?... No, Unc, we won't get ourselves killed and we will take care of our little sisters... Yes, Unc, including Debra... Yes, sir, we know you love her as well as the others.... Yes, sir... Yes, sir, we understand... Yes, sir, we will be careful. Unc? Do us a favor and keep the men and women in blue at bay until we give the signal; we don't want anyone else getting hurt or killed... The signal? You will know when you no longer hear any commotion... Will do, Unc, will do... Can't wait to see you either... So long to you too, Unc... Yes, we love you too... Okay, see you later after this mess is all over with... See you later, goodbye." Greta hung up the phone.

"God damn that man can talk, no wonder he won re-election," Greta said smiling.

"Unc? Unc? Why the hell didn't you tell us that the mayor is your uncle?"

"Well, he really isn't our blood uncle. Ever since Daddy adopted us he's been our uncle, like he's your godfather," Greta finished with a mischievous grin on her face.

"Okay, that's it; let's kick their asses right here and now," Christina said smiling as the four women jumped their two older sisters.

•   •   •   •

Ida M. Pace High School, 7:30 P.M.:

"Okay, the mayor has all four of the entrances locked-up and guarded; no one gets in, no one gets out," Gail told her sisters. "You know the plan, you four split up. Tiny, you walk up the south stairwell to the second floor. Crissy, you go up the north stairwell to the third floor. Deb, you take the east stairwell to the fourth floor. 'J' you take the west stairwell to the fifth floor. Greta, you take the north elevator to the sixth floor. I'll take the south elevator to the third floor. I will wait for you to finish sweeping your floor and then you come to the third floor. If any of the Correctors do show their faces while I'm waiting for you, I will blow my whistle twice. Once all of us are in position, blow your whistle one short burst, and then start searching every room, nook, and cranny."

"Gail? Won't that let them know that someone is here?" Debra asked puzzled.

"Deb, they already know we're here," Gail answered.

"Now remember, the first encounter with any member of the Correctors, press the button on your wrist bracelet, got it? Whoever encounters one of them first, another will come to your aid, needed or not. Do not be a hero; if you encounter more than one, scream like hell then run to the third floor if you can. Any questions?" Gail asked her anxious sisters. No one answered. "Good, we now have three hours before this place gets crowded with people. We have to find the Correctors before then, or the newly-elected mayor will be the first mayor in office who wasn't able to take his seat and this city will be torn apart."

"Why don't we just use the K-9 unit to flush them out?" Justina asked Gail.

"Because we don't want any more officers to get killed, I'm talking about their partners. They will kill both the dog and the officer with him."

"Gail, Greta, we gave you a good description of those women and the only man, Leo. If you have to, shoot and ask questions later; you do not want to tangle with him," said Tynisha, telling her sisters what to expect if they ran into Leo. "He's big and he's mean as hell; if you get the chance, kill him."

"Tiny, don't worry, I'm no picnic myself," Gail assured her little sister. "Besides, he better hope he doesn't run into Greta first; she's the crazy one in the family."

"Another 'J' huh?" Christina said grinning. All the sisters laughed as Justina nudged Christina.

"Okay, let's do this," Greta told her sisters.

"May God be with us," Debra said, as the women split up.

•　　•　　•　　•

As Tynisha reached the second floor, she approached the first door she came to on her left, and blew her whistle. *That's enough to wake up the dead* she thought. A sign on the door read UTILITY CLOSET. Tynisha pulled out her service weapon and slowly opened the door. "Oh!" Tynisha screamed as she was forced backwards to the floor from a powerful front straight kick to her forehead. Lying on her back, still holding her service weapon, Tynisha tried to shake off the effects of the kick. Tynisha then felt the pain in her hand from someone kicking the gun out of it.

"Hello there, we meet again."

Tynisha's eyes slowly recovered from the blurred vision, her eyes came into focus to see Gemini standing over her. "I'm going to kick your yellow ass!" Gemini screamed as she lifted her left leg up to come down on Tynisha's face.

"I'm not handcuffed this time, Aunt 'T'," Tynisha said, as she spun on her back, knocking Gemini off her feet with a leg sweep.

Gemini landed hard on her buttocks, falling back, hitting her head against a wall locker. "Oh," Gemini said, as she grabbed the back of her head.

"Aunt Teresa, you are under arrest; you have the right to remain silent," Tynisha said, as she grabbed her aunt by the back of her hair, telling her to get up. "You have the right..." Tynisha was cut off by the sharp pain in her stomach, as Gemini delivered a back half kick. Bent over in pain, Tynisha felt a blow to her left ribs from a roundhouse kick. Tynisha knew that one or more of her ribs were broken, but had to ignore the pain if she was to survive. Starting to breathe hard, Tynisha backed up and stood facing her aunt. "I'm glad you are making this hard, Aunt 'T'," Tynisha said, as a small trickle of blood came out of her mouth. "Now I don't have to hold back because of the love I have for you because you're my aunt.

The comment seemed to anger Gemini, as she yelled at her niece. "Love? Love for me? You stupid ass, how the hell can you love me when all I did was to beat on you while you were handcuffed? How, stupid ass, how?"

"I know why you did it, Aunt 'T'. You did it to keep Ms. Cancer from killing me, that's why you did it. It's all over Aunt Teresa, all of it is over. Please give up, ple..."

Tynisha's sentence was cut short by a bullet slamming into her lower right side. The bullet slipped past the bulletproof vest she was wearing. Tynisha screamed, grabbing her side, as she fell to the floor.

Gemini screamed, "Aries, no! No, Aries! Don't kill her," as she backed up to her wounded niece, shielding her with her body. "Don't kill..." Gemini's plea was cut short, as the bullet ripped into her left shoulder.

Tynisha screamed, "Noo! Noo!" Tynisha heard the sound of a female's voice, laughing as she watched her aunt fall backwards, landing on top of her.

Gemini picked herself off her niece and holding her hand over her shoulder, began to stagger down the hall, yelling, "Damn you, Aries!" as she disappeared from her niece's sight.

"Aries, my sisters are going to kill you, bitch! Do you hear me? They are going to kill you!" Tynisha yelled down the now empty hallway. Tynisha pressed the button on her silver, diamond-studded bracelet. *I wonder if they are real*, she was thinking to herself, looking at the studs as she grimaced from the pain.

•   •   •   •

"Oh damn, damn, damn! Hold on, little sister," Gail said, as she tore off a strip of cloth from her blouse. Gail placed the strip on her sister's side where the quarter-inch hole was slowly seeping blood.

"How bad is it?" Tynisha asked.

"I-I don't know," Gail said through tears.

"She stood in front of me."

"What?"

"She stood in front of me and took the second bullet that was meant for me," Tynisha said.

"Who took a bullet for you?"

"Aunt Teresa."

"Are you sure?" Gail asked. "Maybe she just got in the line of fire by accident. Besides, why would she take a bullet for you?"

"Because I told her that I love her," Tynisha answered, as she passed out.

"Is she dead?" Greta asked, as she kneeled down over her little sister.

"No, she just passed out." Gail noticed the blood trail leading down the hall.

"Where did she get hit?"

"In the side. She said Aunt Teresa took a bullet that was meant for her. You believe that?"

"Don't know what to believe at this point in time, Gail," Greta answered somberly. Where is Aunt Teresa now?" Greta asked.

"Tiny said she staggered down the hall, she's wounded. Tiny said she was hit in the shoulder. Can you stay with her while I go see about the others and see if I can find Aunt Teresa?"

"Yeah, go ahead, I'll keep my eyes on her and try to slow the bleeding," Greta answered, through falling tears. "If you find Aunt 'T', don't kill her; let's just bring her in alive, if we can."

"I'll try my best, Greta."

"Gail, if you find any of the other Correctors, kill them, kill them on sight."

Gail looked at her sister and said, "You know we can't do that, we are cops, Greta."

"So was my baby sister. Besides, I'm now on vacation, and so are you. Kill them, kill them all."

Gail looked at the stern, cold-blooded expression on her sister's face. "I will, Greta, I will." Gail stood up, walked down the hallway, and disappeared.

Five minutes passed and Greta was getting frustrated, because she couldn't slow down the flow of blood from her little sister's wound. "Damn!" Greta said in disgust, as she felt the cold steel pressed against the back of her right ear.

"Do not make any sudden moves or I will lay your soul to rest," Aries told Greta. "Now slowly with your left hand, take your piece out and shove it down the hall, now." Greta did as she was told.

"Both of them," Aries said in a stern voice. Greta pulled her backup gun from her left ankle holster and threw it down the hall.

"Who are you and why are you here?" Greta said nothing. "Listen to me and listen well. I can blow your damn brains out or we can help my girl…"

"Your girl? Your girl? As far as I know, you may be the one who put her in this position."

"Not me, I would never hurt Tynisha. I like Tynisha, even if she has sworn to bring me in, dead or alive. Now, one more time, who are you?" Aries asked Greta with a tone of anger in her voice.

"She's my sister Greta, Ms. Aries," Tynisha answered.

"Sister? She's not in our files."

"Neither is my sister Gail, but here we are," Greta snapped.

Aries just looked at Greta with contempt in her eyes. "Tynisha, I didn't shoot you, I want to help you. Can I trust your sister not to do anything stupid if I do?"

"To save my sister's life, I give you my word."

Aries looked at Greta for a long hard minute, then put her 9-mm Glock pistol in her right-hand gun holster. "There's a nurse's station down the hall. You get her arms and I'll get her legs, we'll carry her down there."

After picking Tynisha up and starting to carry her the twenty yards to the nurse's office, Greta asked, "Why?"

"Why what?" Aries asked.

"Why are you trying to help the one you put a bullet into?"

"It wasn't me, it was Cancer. Cancer would put a bullet in her mother if she didn't like her, or had a contract on her."

"You don't act like a hired assassin to me, what assassin helps their wounded prey?"

"Listen, lady, I already told you I didn't shoot Tynisha. Think about it, lady, When I walked up on you and you felt that cold steel, did I have the chance of putting a bullet in you and your sister's brains?"

"Yes, you did, so why didn't you?"

"Tracy," Tynisha answered weakly.

"Tracy? What does Tracy have to do with this?"

"She shouldn't have died," Aries answered.

"Well, according to my father, neither should Scorpio," Greta replied.

"True," Aries said.

The trio reached the nurse's station without any more comment.

"We can lay her on the gurney over there," Greta told Aries.

After laying Tynisha down, Aries came up to Tynisha's face and asked her, "Do you trust me, Tynisha?"

"Yes, Ms. Aries, I do," Tynisha answered with a weak smile on her face.

"Good."

"You can call me "Tiny," Tynisha interrupted.

Aries smiled. "Tiny, we are going to have to get that bullet out, or you will either die or be in a wheel chair for the rest of your life. I am a registered nurse, and you are going to have to trust me with your life. Listen, Tiny, when I start digging into your side, you are going to feel pain like you never felt before. You will pass out from it, but it has to be done, girlfriend. Are you ready?"

"Yes, girlfriend, I'm ready," Tynisha answered with a smile. That's when Greta noticed the water build up in Aries' eyes.

• • • •

Christina was halfway down the hall when she got the feeling that someone was watching her. Christina stopped and turned around to find Cancer standing in the hallway with a 9-mm in her right hand, holding it at her side.

"What do you prefer, Christina? Gunfight at the OK Corral, or should we find out if your dead father did a good job teaching you? Your choice," Cancer said smiling.

"Let's see if my dad did a good job," Christina said with a smile on her face.

"Great," Cancer said, as she bent her knees to lay her weapon on the ground. "Here are the rules: We leave our weapons down at our end of the hallway, and when and if either has had enough of getting their ass beat, they can always make a break for their piece, okay?"

"Fine," Christina said, "but no vests."

"Ohhh, I like that—living to the brink, love it," Cancer said, as she opened up her shirt to take off her bulletproof vest.

Christina backed up to her end of the hall and laid her weapon on the floor. Unknown to Cancer, Christina had cocked the 9-mm, ready to be fired.

After Christina had taken off her vest, the two women started running toward each other, colliding in the center of the hall. The impact sent both women to the floor. Both shaken, Christina jumped up off the floor into a full combat-ready stance with her left foot in front and her right crossed behind it, forming a 'T' shape, with her knees bent. Christina's arms are stretched out with both fists balled tight.

Cancer laughed as she advanced toward Christina, flaying her hands in a knife position left to right, screaming. Christina didn't move an inch as her adversary advanced toward her. As Cancer came within three feet in front of Christina, Christina advanced and sent a roundhouse kick to Cancer's head. Cancer ducked the kick and moved into Christina's chest space and delivered a heart-stopping punch to her sternum. Christina backed off feeling her sternum. Christina winced from the pain, as Cancer laughed. Christina kept her cool. Cancer then jumped, spun around, and threw her right leg, catching Christina flush on her chin, sending her to the floor.

"Aw, come on, Christina, I know you can do better than that." Cancer then turned her back and started walking down to her end of the hall toward her weapon.

"Oh, no you don't, bitch!" Christina yelled, getting up off the floor.

Cancer turned around just in time to catch the full force of Christina's flying jump kick to her chest and stomach, knocking her sideways into three lockers. The move stunned Cancer, as she tried desperately to shake off the vicious attack. Cancer then felt her head being rocked left to right from the blows being delivered to the sides and the front of her face from Christina's punches. Cancer tried to move from the vicious attack, but Christina pulled her back, continuing the onslaught. Cancer, bleeding from the mouth, nose, and the corner of both eyes from the assault, bent and threw two balled fists into Christina's solar plexus.

Christina bent over in pain and bit her tongue from the force of Cancer's bending knee kick to her chin, knocking her backward to the floor. Dazed, Christina felt the pain from the first kick to her stomach, then the second, the third, and fourth. Christina felt herself trying to blackout, but fought off the feeling.

As Cancer lifted her right leg to deliver a stomp to Christina's side, Christina kicked Cancer in the groin. Cancer fell to the floor. With Cancer bent over in pain with her left hand cupped over her crotch, and her right holding her abdomen, she heard, "You have the right to remain silent, you have the right to an..."

"Shut the fuck up," Christina was cut off by Cancer, as she put a handcuff on her right wrist and pulled the other cuff around a covered steam pipe and then cuffed her left wrist.

"Stay put," Christina said, as she walked down the hall to retrieve her weapon, holding her right side, rubbing her chest, and spitting out blood from her torn tongue.

"One of these days, I'm going to kill you bitch!" Cancer screamed at Christina, fading away down the dimly lit corridor.

"By the way, Ms. Cancer, Daddy isn't dead."

"I'm going to kill the both of you bitches!" Cancer screamed.

•　　•　　•　　•

"Ms. Libra? Ms. Libra? Come out, come out wherever you are," Justina said, as she walked down the long hall, carrying her 9-mm in her right hand at her side, checking every classroom she passed. Justina's blood ran cold, as she looked up at a round stainless steel hall mirror and spotted Libra walking up behind her with her weapon in her outstretched right hand, aimed at her back. Justina walked past the mirror, as if she hadn't seen it and, again, called out Libra's name. "Ms. Libra, come out, come out wherever you are."

Still, Libra said nothing. Justina's heart started racing when she heard Libra cock the chamber on her weapon. "Guess what, Ms. Libra, peek-a-boo, I see you." Justina dropped and spun around, catching Libra off guard and fired in her direction. Justina heard Libra's weapon fire, then felt the impact to her chest. Justina fell backwards, as the bullet slammed into her bulletproof vest. "Hot damn, that hurts," Justina said, as she lifted her pain racked torso to sit up. "Thank God for those old western movies." Justina then looked down the hall to see Libra sitting up against a windowsill with her lower jaw blown away. "Damn, that's even gross to me."

•   •   •   •

Gail heard the gunfire and started running to each floor, looking down the hall-way of each. As Gail reached the third, she saw Christina sitting on the stairs, holding her side. Seeing her, Christina smiled. "Is it over, yet?" Christina asked.

"Don't know," Gail answered. "Are you alright?"

"No, that crazy bitch tried to stomp me to death."

"Where is she?"

"Come on, I'll show you," Christina said, as she stood up and started walking.

"So, you're Cancer," Gail said, as she approached Cancer. "Pleased to meet you. Uncle Sam has been looking for you a very long time."

"Go fu..." Cancer was cut off by a punch to her chin. Cancer's eyes rolled to the back of her head as she passed out.

"Did that feel good?" Christina asked Gail.

"Yep, later on I'll have one for myself; that one was for my baby sister."

"Come on, let's go find Justina," Christina said. "I just heard gunfire upstairs."

Gail and Christina ran up the next flight of stairs, down the hallway, and looked to their left to find Libra along the windowsill.

"Damn, I just hope 'J' got off the first shot," Gail said, looking at Libra, who had her eyes wide open, as if in shock.

The two women heard footsteps coming down the hallway; they both spun around with their guns to the ready. "Slow down, slow down, you two better start drinking coffee, no caffeine." It was Justina, walking down the hall, rub-bing her chest.

"It looks like she didn't want to give up," Christina said smiling at Justina, looking at Libra.

"The bitch tried to bushwhack me, didn't work," Justina said without any expression on her face. Where are Greta, Tynisha, and Deb?" Justina asked.

"I left Greta with Tiny on the next floor. Tiny's been hit in the side," Gail answered somberly.

All three women heard the heart-shattering scream from upstairs. "Oh shit, that's Deb," Christina said, as the three women raced to the stairwell.

"Go ahead and scream all you want, little lady," Leo said, as he punched Debra on the right side of her now badly swollen face. "You put up a good fight, I give you that much," Leo said, wiping his ripped, torn, and bleeding face. "Now, is there anything you want to say before you die?" Leo said, looking down on the broken and beaten body of the young woman. Picking Debra up, Debra looked Leo straight in the face and smiled through her cracked, swollen, bloody lips. "What the hell are you smiling about?" Leo asked his half-dead prey.

"Your death," Debra said, as her eyes looked beyond Leo to the back of the hall.

Leo let go of Debra's collar and turned in the direction of her eyes. Debra fell to the floor. Leo was shocked to see Gail, Christina, and Justina standing in the hall with their guns in hand, pointed directly at him. "Oh shit," Leo said, as he reached and pulled his weapon from his waistband and started to raise it up. Without saying a word, the trio opened fire. Leo twitched and turned as the nine bullets smashed into, and mangled his huge frame. The women stopped firing, as Leo's torn body hit the floor in a heap. The trio of women looked down at Leo's heavily ripped up torso as he inhaled and exhaled for the last time.

Debra tried to stand up, but fell back down. "A hand anyone?" she said, peering through her half swollen, good left eye. Debra's right eye was swollen shut.

The sisters smiled and shook their heads. Even after getting half the life beaten out of her, she still has a sense of humor. Gail said, looking at her little sister smiling, "Let's go and get Greta and Tiny."

All three women gently picked up the broken and swollen body of their sister and carried her down the steps. "Damn, where are they?" Gail asked out loud when they reached the second floor hallway.

"Hell, you tell us," Christina said, looking at a blood trail.

Looking down at the floor, Justina said, "Let's just follow it." The four women follow the trail to the nurse's station, where they peered through the glass to find Greta giving Aries a big hug. The women opened the door and walked in.

Greta screamed, "Oh, my god," looking at Debra.

"It's not as bad as it looks," Debra said through a half smile.

"Put her on that gurney," Aries said (pointing to a wall on their left), coming over to Debra. The women said nothing, but did as Aries had asked.

"I thought everyone was evacuated from the building?" Gail asked Greta.

"They were."

"So who's the candy striper?"

"Her name is Ms. Aries and she just saved my life, big sis," Tynisha said, lifting her head up. Gail was shocked.

"There's not much I can do for your sister here. She has a broken leg, multiple broken ribs, and the reason she's not bleeding a lot on the outside is because she's bleeding internally. You've got to get her to a hospital and fast," Aries said, holding out both her wrists.

Gail looked at her. "What the hell am I supposed to do with you now?" Gail asked.

"I can't answer that for you, you have to answer that yourself," Aries said. "Look, if you let me go, the people who hired us will hunt me and the rest of the Correctors down and kill us. With you turning me in, my life lasts only as long as the appeals hold out; either way I'm dead."

Tynisha lifted up her body and said, "If it wasn't for Ms. Aries, Aunt Teresa would have used me for her personal punching bag."

"But, didn't you say that Aunt Teresa took a bullet for you?" Gail asked.

"Yes, she did, after the fact. I took the first one."

"Then Aries saved your life a second time? What are you, Irish?" Debra asked Tynisha smiling.

"I'm not turning her in or letting her go out there by herself," Tynisha said. "Now, if the people who hired her want her, then they are going to have to come through me to get her; it's as simple as that," Tynisha concluded.

"I'm not doing it either," Greta said, backing up Tynisha.

"You know, she does have a point there," Justina added to the conversation. "I will not give up a person who just saved my sister's life, Gail," Justina said. "Who we should be pissed off at are the people who hired the Correctors in the first place. The way I see it, it wasn't the Correctors who killed our baby sister, it was the people who hired them," Justina concluded.

"So, what you are saying is, we've got issues with the people who hired the Correctors and not Ms. Red Cross over here?" Gail asked.

"Yes," all the sisters answered all at once.

"We'll deal with that issue when it comes around," Gail said.

"The ball is on your side of the court, Gail," Debra interjected.

"Okay, okay, how the hell do we do this? How the hell do we get her past the mayor and the cops?" Greta asked.

"She was locked into a locker and we heard her screaming for help," Christina said smiling.

"No, that's not going to work, the mayor's not stupid," Gail said.

"Look, whatever we are going to do, we better hurry up and do it, because they just stormed the school," Tynisha said.

"It's plain and simple; all you tell them is she is our cousin, who was standing by if we needed her and we did," Debra said grinning.

"Shit, Mom and Daddy are going to kill us," Gail said smiling. "Well, the only thing I can say is…," Gail stopped and looked at her sisters for approval. All the sisters nodded their heads with approval, "welcome to the family, Aries. I guess we have an extra bedroom," Gail said, holding her hand out.

"It's Kimberly, I prefer Kim, and I snore," Aries said smiling, as she shook Gail's hand.

"Oh God, Daddy is just going to love this shit. We are dead," Justina said smiling. All the sisters started laughing.

"Has anyone seen Aunt Teresa?" Gail asked.

"Not us," Greta answered for herself, Tynisha, and Aries.

"Hell, I can't see at all, let alone see Aunt Teresa," Debra said smiling.

"Not me," Christina said.

"Not I," Justina added.

"Shit, damn it all," Gail said.

"Look, Gail, if Aunt Teresa can get past the mayor and all the cops out here, then she deserves to get away. Besides, we'll get her the next time around," Christina said.

"The next time around? The next time around? Hell we just about got out of this alive and you are talking about the next time around?" Justina yelled at Christina. All the women laughed

THE END?

CPSIA information can be obtained
at www.ICGtesting.com
Printed in the USA
BVHW042325190620
581826BV00009B/295